STAGE FRIGHT

NANCY DREW
girl detective*

THE HARDY BOYS
UNDERCOVER BROTHERS*

Available from Aladdin

GIRL DETECTIVE®

NANCY DREW
AND THE
UNDERCOVER BROTHERS®
HARDY BOYS
Super Mystery #6

STAGE FRIGHT

CAROLYN KEENE
and
FRANKLIN W. DIXON

Aladdin

NEW YORK LONDON TORONTO SYDNEY NEW DELHI

ALADDIN

An imprint of Simon & Schuster Children's Publishing Division

1230 Avenue of the Americas, New York, NY 10020

First Aladdin paperback edition July 2012

Copyright © 2012 by Simon & Schuster, Inc.

All rights reserved, including the right of reproduction in whole or in part in any form.

ALADDIN is a trademark of Simon & Schuster, Inc., and related logo is
a registered trademark of Simon & Schuster, Inc.

NANCY DREW and colophon are registered trademarks of Simon & Schuster, Inc.

NANCY DREW: GIRL DETECTIVE is a trademark of Simon & Schuster, Inc.

THE HARDY BOYS MYSTERY STORIES is a trademark of Simon & Schuster, Inc.

HARDY BOYS UNDERCOVER BROTHERS and related logo are registered
trademarks of Simon & Schuster, Inc.

For information about special discounts for bulk purchases,
please contact Simon & Schuster Special Sales at 1-866-506-1949 or
business@simonandschuster.com.

The Simon & Schuster Speakers Bureau can bring authors to your live event.

For more information or to book an event contact the
Simon & Schuster Speakers Bureau at 1-866-248-3049 or
visit our website at www.simonspeakers.com.

Designed by Sammy Yuen Jr.

The text of this book was set in Meridien.

Manufactured in the United States of America 0612 OFF

2 4 6 8 10 9 7 5 3 1

Library of Congress Control Number 2012933198

ISBN 978-1-4424-5681-5

ISBN 978-1-4424-5682-2 (eBook)

CONTENTS

CHAPTER 1

JOE

LUCK O' THE IRISH

"Canya dew any bett'r?" said Frank. Listening to him, I had to admit I was impressed. His Irish accent was impossible to understand. That afternoon he had spent watching and rewatching *The Commitments* had paid off.

We were sitting in the small backroom of a gas station on the western coast of Ireland, across a wide wooden table from three men who couldn't have looked more like stereotypical Irish gangsters if they tried. Each guy was shorter, skinnier, and tougher looking than the next. All three wore brown newsboy caps. They looked so much alike they had to be brothers, or a father and two sons, or a grandfather, father, and son. The only way I could tell them apart was their hair. In my head, I'd dubbed them "Black," "Gray," and "Salt-'n'-Pepper."

They huddled together and whispered furiously. Then Salt-'n'-Pepper turned back to us.

"No," he said.

"Yer a man of few words," I said. "I loik that in a fella."

No one said a thing. *So much for that famous "gift o' the gab" the Irish are supposed to have,* I thought.

"Right ye are then," said Frank. "A mil."

He pulled a small bag from beneath his chair and popped the lid, showing the neat stacks of euros, one atop the other, inside—or rather, four neat stacks of just euros and beneath them four more stacks, one of which also held a tracking device. Once this sale was complete, these guys would be going to jail for a good long time. We just had to get one thing out of harm's way first.

Black picked up a stack of euros and flipped through them, making sure they were real. Then he nodded to Salt-'n'-Pepper, who pulled a medium-sized black box out from behind him. He placed it on the table and slowly removed the lid to reveal a two-foot tall, incredibly delicate gold statue of a woman—a woman with six arms! Her lips were curled in a snarl, and a chain of skulls hung around her neck. It was gross and cool all at the same time. I decided it would make the best Halloween costume ever—if I were a girl, that was. What was it the briefing had called her? Kali! "An Indian goddess in charge of time, and change, and death." She was definitely hard-core.

"Whoa!" I said as I admired the statue. "That is awwwwwe-some."

Salt-'n'-Pepper froze. Frank kicked me under the table.

"Uh . . . I mean . . . brill?" I tried to cover, but it didn't work. I could see it on their faces. Our cover was blown.

Salt-'n'-Pepper slammed the cover back down over the statue, but Frank grabbed it by the base and yanked it out from under him. Black and Gray were getting to their feet, reaching inside their jackets for something. I was pretty sure they weren't about to offer me a piece of gum.

I kicked up as hard as I could. The heel of my boot caught the table by the edge and flipped it over, sending it slamming down hard on the toes of Black and Gray. They howled in shock. A million euros were suddenly flying through the air. Black was hopping on one leg and trying to grab the money with his free hand, while Gray was on his knees, cradling his foot.

"Git 'em!" screamed Salt-'n'-Pepper. "We been had!"

"Window!" I yelled to Frank.

Thankfully, we'd already scoped out the exits before we even got to the meet. The gas station was a front. The clerk behind the counter? She was an assassin on Interpol's most-wanted list. Going back out the door we came through was a one-way ticket—and not back to Bayport. But the small window on the other side of the room seemed to be just wide enough for us. Or at least, for me. Frank had been eating a lot of junk food recently and . . .

Smash!

Frank hit the window like a football quarterback aiming for a touchdown, his body curled protectively around the statue of Kali. The glass, the frame, and part of the wall exploded outward in a rain of shrapnel. I was right behind him. And right behind me was Salt-'n'-Pepper.

Bam! Bam! Bam!

"I thought they didn't have guns over here!" I yelled, as we ducked and wove across a long grassy field.

"The police don't!" Frank yelled back. "But no one said anything about the criminals. Here, catch!"

Frank tossed Kali up in the air. She shimmered in the sunlight as she spun end over end. I squinted, my vision blurred by the bright light, but Frank's aim was perfect. All I had to do was open my hand, and Kali fell right into it.

"Good throw!" I yelled to Frank, holding the statue aloft. Then a bullet nearly took one of her six arms off, and I stuffed her into a specially designed pocket inside my coat. I glanced back. Salt-'n'-Pepper was pretty spry for his age! He wasn't far behind us. And in front of us . . .

"Uh, Frank?" I said. "I think we have a problem."

Frank was silent. I looked over at him. He'd swung his backpack around to his front, like all the Spanish high school tourists did at the airport. He was fiddling with it somehow, and it looked like the bag was starting to come apart in his hands. I could see the metal rods that made up its frame, and something heavy and black inside it. Now was so not the time for fabric origami.

Bam! Salt-'n'-Pepper took another potshot at us, but I guess he'd realized he didn't need to shoot us. We were running out of options—literally.

"Frank? Hey! FRANK!" I yelled. "Look up."

Finally, Frank did. We were thirty feet from the edge of one of the biggest cliffs I'd ever seen in my life. It plunged straight down into the ocean, hundreds of feet below. And it extended as far as I could see in either direction! Salt-'n'-Pepper had us trapped.

"Yeah, what?" was Frank's nonchalant response. "They're the Cliffs of Moher. They're famous." He returned to fiddling with his bag, which now looked like some sort of mutant half backpack, half kite.

"Well right now, they're famously in our way! We have to . . . What's that?"

Frank's bag no longer looked anything like a backpack. In fact, it looked like a hang glider. The metal frame of the bag had become the frame of the glider, the fabric was the wings, and the metal box was . . . a weird metal box attached at the top.

"It's an ultralight!" Frank replied. "Didn't you read the briefing notes?"

"No!" I yelled back. The cliffs were maybe ten feet away, and at the rate we were running, we only had a few seconds before we went over. "And now isn't the time to lecture me about it!"

"Grab on!" Frank replied, holding the ultralight in front of him.

Without any other options, I did as he said. Hands latched on the frame of the ultralight, we ran right off the edge of the cliff. The wind plucked us up, and suddenly we were gliding out over the crashing waves below.

"Great!" I yelled at Frank. "But what do we do now? This thing isn't going to stay in the air long—not with both of us hanging from it."

Frank had strapped himself to the bar before we jumped so he could reach up and flick a switch on the small black box at the center of the ultralight. A tiny motor kicked on, and we leapt upward. Suddenly, this whole ultralight thing became a lot cooler.

Bam! Fssst!

A bullet ripped through the left wing of the ultralight, throwing us into a tight slide to the left. I grabbed Frank's shoulder with my free arm and we clung to the ultralight with all our might. We dropped ten feet in two seconds, like a plane in heavy turbulence, before the ultralight found a new updraft and recovered.

I peered behind us. Salt-'n'-Pepper was standing at the edge of the cliffs, jumping up and down with frustration.

"Careful!" I yelled back at him. "You don't want to fall in!"

I stared out at the ocean. Away from the cliffs, the water was smooth as glass. We were surrounded by a million shades of blue—the water, the sky, even the clouds seemed tinged with blue. I could get used to this!

"You know, the meeting point makes a lot more sense now," I said to Frank, as we flew swiftly out to sea.

"Ha!" replied Frank. "Someday, you're going to read an entire mission briefing, and I'm going to drop dead from shock."

"I would never do that to you . . . promise." I smiled at Frank. "Hey, look!"

A small blue ship had appeared on the horizon, flying a pirate flag with two crossed video-game joysticks below it. It was maybe twenty feet long and would have been pretty difficult to land a hang glider on, if we weren't the two awesomest spies in the world.

"That must be Vijay!" I yelled, as a small figure waved at us. Vijay was another member of American Teens Against Crime. He was a field agent, like us, but he mostly handled the tech side of things. Our job in this mission was to rescue Kali, his was to make sure she got back to her rightful owner, the National Museum of India.

"Taking us down," said Frank. Carefully, we shifted our weight back and forth, slowly guiding the ultralight down. Below us, the deck of the ship got bigger and bigger. Vijay was there, standing next to a big red fishing pole whose line was bobbing in the water. Behind him was an open hatch that led belowdecks. Aside from that it was just warm sun, cool breezes, and perfect blue water. A guy could get used to this!

"Hey guys," said Vijay, as we landed on the deck with a thump. "Yes!" he yelled suddenly, pumping his fist in the air. "Twenty–pound rainbow trout, for the win!" He waved a black handheld video game in the air.

"Are you playing a fishing game?" I asked, as Frank began dismantling the ultralight. "You're standing on a boat in the middle of the Atlantic Ocean. Next to a fishing pole! Why don't you actually, like, fish?"

Vijay shot me a cold look.

"One," he said. "Do you know how hard it is to catch fish in the ocean? The ocean is big, my friend. The fish? Small. Very small."

He paused to slip the game system back into the pocket of his jacket. Then he picked up the fishing pole and began reeling the line in.

"Two," Vijay continued. "Look at these hands. Do you know how much they're worth? ATAC insured my hands for a million dollars last year. Or did you think that ultralight made itself?"

The fishing line reached the surface of the water, but instead of a hook, there was a metal sphere at the end of it. Vijay picked it up, removed a key from his pocket, and opened the top of the sphere to reveal a waterproof chamber inside.

"Three, this fishing pole is really just a docking station for a homing submersible I built last week, which will get this"—Vijay paused and plucked the statue of Kali from me—"all the way back to India without sending it through the mob-controlled Irish customs department."

Vijay slipped Kali into the sphere, where she fit perfectly. Then he flipped the lid back down and turned the key all the way around in the lock twice. A small blue light appeared on the top of the sphere, and somewhere inside it a motor began running.

"Want to do the honors?" Vijay asked, holding the sphere out to us.

"You go for it," Frank said. I took the sphere in my hands. It weighed barely more than the statue alone. I hefted it high. I glanced at Vijay, just to make sure. He nodded, and I threw the submersible as hard as I could through the air. It landed with a splash, bobbed in the water for a second, and then rapidly motored away.

"So that's it?" I asked, sitting down on the deck. "We're done here?"

"Yup," said Frank as he joined me. "Go team! As a reward, I say we stay here for the rest of the weekend."

Vijay cleared his throat. I knew from the sound that he didn't have good news.

"Sorry guys, I have to send you back out on a mission. But there is a silver lining. . . ." Vijay raced below decks and came up with a large pizza box.

"Give it here!" I yelled, scrambling for the pizza. Missions have a way of making me hungry.

I flipped open the lid and there was a piping hot, fresh pizza covered in sausage and onions—my favorite.

"How do you do that?" I asked. Vijay often hid our missions inside pizzas, and somehow, no matter where we were, his pizzas were always fresh and hot. If I wasn't certain before, I knew it now: Vijay was a genius.

"Shhh!" responded Vijay. "Trade secret. If you knew, I'd have to kill you. Now check out the screen on top."

I looked at the lid of the pizza box. Sure enough, inside the top was a flat screen TV! Frank scraped some cheese off the glass and we sat down to watch.

"This is Claire Cleveland," the narration began, showing a photo of a pretty girl with long brown hair.

"Oh, I know her!" Frank yelled out. "She's on that show, *Joy!*"

"Claire is the star of the hit musical show, *Joy!*" continued the narrator, and I whacked Frank on the shoulder to get him to be quiet. "She's also set to star in a new Broadway musical, *Wake*, which tells the story of one of World War II's most decorated female spies, Nancy Wake. The show opens this week—or at least it will, if the two of you are able to stop the mysterious accidents that have plagued the show throughout rehearsals."

A blond man and woman—obviously related—appeared on the screen. They were young, richly dressed, and seemed too perfect looking to be real.

"This is the brother-and-sister Broadway team behind *Wake*—Laurel and Linden von Louden. Last night Linden called ATAC for help. It seems the 'accidents' have been getting worse, and as of last night, he has confirmation that they aren't really accidents."

A new shot appeared on the screen, a close-up of a cell phone. Across the screen, in big letters, was a text message that read "You will die here!!!!!"

I bit down hard in surprise, and the pizza burned the roof of my mouth, badly.

"Ow!" I mumbled, trying to stay focused on the briefing.

"This message was sent to Claire late last night," said the narrator. "Claire refuses to go on without adequate protection. This is where the two of you come in. It's up to the two of you to make sure the curtain goes up without a hitch. Good luck, boys."

The screen went blank.

"So . . . does that mean we don't get to spend the weekend on the boat?"

A strange noise began to grow in the distance, a sort of *whump-whump-whump* sound.

"'Fraid not," said Vijay. "In fact, I'd scarf that pizza down quick, because unless someone else called the helicopter taxi service, that's your ride!"

I noticed a distant dot on the horizon starting to grow bigger. I looked at Frank. He nodded at me. Together, we reached down and grabbed a slice of pizza in each hand. I looked back at the helicopter. It was maybe two minutes away.

"We got this under control," I said. Then Frank and I fist-bumped our pizza-filled hands and laughed.

Spy life was the sweet life, for sure.

CHAPTER **2**

NANCY

THE WRONG WAY

"Drive!" I yelled at Bess, as I ran full speed toward my car, a sky-blue drop-top convertible hybrid. Bess was just shifting out of park as I leapt into the backseat.

"They're right behind me!" I yelled. "Get us out of here!"

Bess peeled out of the parking space like a cheetah on fire. Behind us came the sound of doors slamming and men shouting. It was nighttime, and their loud voices echoed through the empty parking lot. The Cross County Galleria Plaza, River Heights' newest mall, was set to open in six weeks. Until that time, it was a haven for skateboarders, kids with nothing to do on a Thursday afternoon, and local government officials looking to take bribes in order to vote a certain way. Can you guess which of the three had Bess, George, and me out there at midnight on a Tuesday?

"Did it work?" asked George from the passenger seat. "Did you get everything?"

I pulled the heavy black plastic glasses off my face. "Oh, it worked all right. I got the lieutenant governor on tape taking the cash in return for his vote on the new oil tax bill. It's all right here," I said, tapping the glasses against the back of her seat. George had built them in her garage, and they contained a pinhole video camera that recorded everything I saw.

"Woohoo!" yelled George, holding her hand up for a high five. I left her hanging.

"But you forgot to mention there was a playback button . . ." I continued. The deal had been finished, the lieutenant governor had his suitcase full of money, and his three goons were just opening the door for me to leave, when I accidentally brushed my hand against the frame of the glasses. Suddenly, our secret deal was projected on the wall, bigger than life and twice as illegal. I hightailed it out the door while they were still standing there stunned.

"Guys, we got a problem," said Bess. I peeked behind us. Sure enough, a black Mercedes with tinted windows was riding up on us. It wasn't hard to guess whose car it was. Aside from the new mall, everything else on this road was corporate office parks and large retail outlets, all of which were closed for the night. If we saw any other cars all evening, I'd be surprised.

"Drive faster!" I yelled. Those bodyguards meant business, and if the bulges in their jackets were any indication, they were carrying some pretty big weapons. Thankfully, Bess was driving my getaway car. She was seriously some sort of car whisperer.

"Sorry about that," said George. "Give them to me and I can upload the video straight to the police server."

I reached out to hand the glasses to George, when suddenly, the Mercedes slammed into the car from behind.

"Ahh!" yelled Bess, as she yanked hard on the wheel, desperately trying to keep us on the road.

"Ow!" I screamed as my hand hit the door. My fingers went numb instantly, and the glasses shot forward out of my hand. "No!" I yelled. If after all that had happened we lost the evidence, it would be a total disaster.

Luckily, the glasses hit the antenna on the hood of the car. The frame hooked onto the antenna, and the glasses spun around like a top before coming to rest at the base. Those glasses were the only proof I had of the lieutenant governor's bribery scheme. I'd been working this case for months. I couldn't afford to blow it now. By morning, I'd bet the lieutenant governor would have covered up his tracks. Either I got those glasses back, or he got off scot-free.

"Avoid them!" I yelled, as I began to clamber into the front seat.

"Easy for you to say," responded Bess. As the Mercedes geared up to ram us again, she tapped the brake and spun the wheel to the right. I slammed into George, but the Mercedes missed us by half an inch.

"Fancy steering, cuz!" laughed George. As usual, I could tell she was enjoying this. If anybody in the world could make this sort of thing fun, it would be Bess and George. We'd been friends for I-don't-know-how-long, and between the three of us we'd gotten out of much tougher situations than this.

But that didn't mean I was going to enjoy what I was about to do.

"Hold her steady," I said as I pulled the belt out of my jeans. I looped it around my left hand and pulled it tight.

"Nancy, what are you doing?" asked George. "I don't like the look of this!"

"Hold this," I said, handing her the other end of my belt. She grabbed it automatically. I took a deep breath and tried to clear my mind. I needed to be focused for this to work.

"I don't think this is—Nancy, stop!"

But it was too late. In one quick motion, I stepped out of the car, over the windshield, and onto the hood. The wind buffeted my face at such high speed that I could barely see. The car rattled and shifted beneath me, and the only thing that kept me from falling was George's grip on my belt.

"Whatever you do, don't let go," I yelled, as I got down on my hands and knees and began to climb across the hood. I tried to tell myself that I'd done way more dangerous things in the past, but at that moment, I couldn't come up with any.

BAM!

The Mercedes slammed us from behind, and for a moment, Bess seemed to lose control. The car fishtailed wildly, and I fell to the side. My left arm was hanging off the edge of the hood, dangling just a few feet above the road. At this speed, the asphalt would feel like a giant cheese grater on my skin.

"Pull!" I yelled, and George did, slowly dragging me back to the center of the hood. Quickly, I snatched the glasses from the antenna. I started climbing back toward the windshield, when suddenly I saw the Mercedes creeping up on us again.

"Bess, speed up!"

Bess slammed her foot down on the gas as hard as she could. The car kicked and bucked, accelerating at a speed that its original manufacturers would never have thought possible. When Bess and George rebuilt my hybrid, they made it the perfect car for the girl detective on the go: fuel efficient, cute, and impossibly fast.

The force of the acceleration rolled me right over the windshield and into George's lap.

"Looking for these?" I asked, holding the glasses up.

"And she gets a perfect ten, folks!" said George, in her best sports announcer voice. "We have a new gymnastic world record."

"Now that you're back with us," said Bess. "I suggest you buckle up and hold on!"

I scooted into the backseat and swung my belt on not a moment too soon. Bess slammed the wheel to the left, sending the car swerving into the entrance ramp for the Sport Time Recreation Center, a popular hangout with arcade games, skee-ball bowling, and a whole bunch of other amusements. Unfortunately, at one a.m. on a Tuesday, it was deserted!

"Bess, what are you doing?" I asked.

"Watch," she said.

The Mercedes, unable to corner quite as fast, shot past us down the street. Bess pumped the gas, swerving the car down the long driveway and parking lot, circling around Sport Time until we were headed for the exit ramp. A hundred yards farther down the street, the Mercedes also turned into the Sport Time exit.

"Bess!" George yelled. "They're cutting us off!"

Indeed, if neither of us swerved, we were hurtling toward a head-on collision with the black Mercedes. I guess that was one way of getting them off our tail. . . .

"Wait for it, wait for it," murmured Bess. The Mercedes sped up, convinced they had us trapped. And as far as I could tell, they did!

Suddenly there was a tremendous popping sound. The Mercedes bucked up in the air and then swerved off the road, its tires flopping around like deflated balloons.

"What the heck?" I asked, as Bess nimbly avoided the stranded Mercedes and shot back out on the highway.

"The sign said no entrance," smiled Bess. "They really should learn to obey the law."

I looked back down the exit ramp. From this angle, I could just barely make out the sharp metal teeth that had ripped the lieutenant governor's wheels right out from under him.

I laughed all the way to the police station.

CHAPTER **3**

FRANK

CRASH AND BURN

Wow, I thought. I'd never seen anything quite so big in my life. It made my head spin. I had to tilt my head back just to get it all. It was one huge skyscraper. And next to it was another. And another. And another.

New York City was amazing. I couldn't help but be impressed every time we visited. And Times Square was probably the most impressive part of all, what with all the people running around and all the bright lights.

"Did you know that Times Square was named for the *New York Times*?" I told Joe, who was standing next to me with his mouth hanging open. "Before that it was called Longacre Square."

I looked over at Joe, whose mouth was still open. "Joe? It's cool, but it's not that cool."

"No," said Joe, shaking his head. "But they are!"

He pointed to the other end of the square, where four supermodels were doing a photo shoot with an old school New York City cab. That was Joe for you.

"You know I read somewhere that for every one hundred people in Manhattan, there's one model?" Joe said. "It's true. I saw it on the Internet. New York has the highest model-to-normal-people ratio."

"Come on," I laughed. "We were supposed to get to the theater at two p.m., and it's already ten after."

We were staying at a hotel not far from the theater, but we'd had some time to kill this morning and we'd done some exploring. Unfortunately, we hadn't counted on the subway taking quite as long as it did to get us back to Times Square. We were supposed to be watching one of the final afternoon rehearsals for *Wake*. The show opened in five days, and Laurel and Linden von Louden wanted us there ASAP.

Wake was in the Matilda Swearson Theatre, which was one of the biggest, oldest, and most beautiful on Broadway. All of the greats had performed there over the years. It was the stage, they said, that could make or break your career. Or in Claire's case, your neck.

It was only a half block off of Times Square, and it was easy to spot.

"Whoa!" said Joe. "What are all these people doing here?"

The theater was a mob scene. There must have been at least fifty, possibly even a hundred teenage fans standing outside. Some had candles. Others held posters proclaiming their love for Claire. One guy had brought a guitar and was singing Claire an original love song. I listened to him for a second. I was pretty sure he'd tried to rhyme Claire with éclair. Not cool.

"They're here for Claire," I told Joe. "I guess she really is as popular as the briefing said."

We'd worked with some celebrities before, but this was pretty off the hook for a Broadway show. It had to be people who loved her TV show, *Joy!* I'd never really watched it, but I'd heard it was about a high school girl who dealt with everything by singing about it. It was the hottest show on television, and her videos had been all over YouTube. There were even three cast albums from the show, all of which had gone gold in their first month!

"We'll just have to push our way through, I guess," said Joe. I couldn't think of any other way in, and so we jumped into the crowd. Boy, were these kids crazy!

"This is worse than that riot in the market in Morocco," I whispered to Joe as we tried to force our way past angry-teen-boy elbows. "These guys are insane!"

"I've been waiting here for two weeks," yelled one guy as we slipped past him. "No cutting!"

"She really brings the crazy out in her fans, doesn't she?" said Joe. I had to agree. And I had to wonder—were we looking at a whole crowd of suspects? Crazy fans did crazy things, as Joe and I knew from experience!

By the time we'd fought our way through the crowd, it was nearly two thirty. The rehearsal would be in full swing already. I hated being late, but there was nothing we could do about it now.

"Hi!" I said to the (very large) security guard who stood between the theater doors and Claire's fans. He was the kind of guy who made refrigerators feel small. "I'm Frank Hardy."

I stuck out my hand, but the security guard ignored it. He stared at me silently. Joe and I must have looked like just two more obsessed fans. Thankfully, he was carrying a clipboard with names on it.

"I . . . think we should be on the list? Laurel and Linden asked us to come here?"

His eyes flicked down to the paper for a millisecond. "Frank and Joe?" he asked. We nodded. He checked our IDs and let us in, without ever looking away from the crowd for more than half a second. This was some tight security.

The lobby of the theater was old New York fantastic: lots of marble and velvet and gold. There was a chandelier more than six feet in diameter. The twin doors that led into the main area of the theater were open, and from inside I could hear music and talking. We were definitely late.

"Shhh," I whispered to Joe. "Let's go in and see."

Even if we had to wait to meet Laurel, Linden, and Claire, it probably couldn't hurt to scope out the place a little. I could already tell this was going to be a hard place to wrap my head around. There were numerous doors leading to various areas of the theater. It made sense, I guess—they needed to move people on and off the stage, and audiences in and out quickly. But it made a bodyguard's life terrible! You never knew where someone might come from or disappear to. Just in the lobby alone, I counted seven doors.

The theater was dark when we entered, though the lights were up on the stage. Joe and I slipped into two seats in the back row and looked around. At the front of the theater I could see a group of five or six people seated together. If I had to bet, I'd say they were Linden, Laurel, and some of their crew.

The stage had probably two dozen people on it, but it was easy to pick out Claire, even at a distance. She was the one standing center stage in a beautiful red dress.

"What can I do?" she sang, in a beautiful low voice. Stacks of *Playbill*s were set up by our seats, and I flipped one open.

Wake *is based on the life of Nancy Wake, a.k.a. the White*

Mouse. During World War II, she was one of the Allies' most feared and trusted secret agents. She was among the most decorated women in the war. She recruited more than 7,000 resistance fighters from occupied territory, pulled off daring raids on prison camps to rescue POWs, and once broke the neck of an SS officer with her bare hands.

"Check this out," I mouthed to Joe, passing him the *Playbill*. "Remind you of someone?"

We met a lot of tough people in our line of work, but when it came to female spies, there was only one Nancy who I put 100 percent of my trust in—Nancy Drew. Someday, I had no doubt, there would be a play about her exploits. Or maybe even a book!

As Joe read the *Playbill*, I watched Claire. A dozen backup dancers dressed in Nazi uniforms were approaching. Aggressively, they twirled and spun and leapt toward her. Cameras projected high-def video of burning houses and flying bullets all around her. Slowly, the Nazis backed her into a corner. My heart started racing. It may not have been an IMAX theater or the new ZOMG Kill game, but this was pretty great stuff.

Or at least, the production *looked* great. The visuals and the set were intense. But the more I watched, the more obvious mistakes I saw the dancers make. And though Claire was performing her heart out, and she looked fantastic, she couldn't keep the whole thing running on her own. Even without knowing the show,

I could tell they were messing up. One was way over on the opposite side of the stage from everyone else. Another seemed to be about three seconds behind the music.

A droning sound started to fill the theater. I looked up.

"Wow!"

My jaw dropped. Three planes were circling the stage and the audience. Their propellers spun and their engines roared. They had bullet holes in the wings, and terrifying shark teeth painted on their cockpits. Although each was only about ten feet long, they looked incredibly realistic. This show had really gone all out on the effects, if not on the actors and dancers.

"What's that smell?" whispered Joe, quietly. "Are you still wearing those shoes from when we escaped that fire in Milwaukee?"

I looked down to check. I didn't think I was, but . . . you never know. Laundry is definitely not my best skill. But no, these were new. I could smell it now too. There was definitely smoke in the air somewhere. But for the life of me, I couldn't see it.

"Maybe it's just a special effect," I whispered back.

"*Wake*!" said Joe. "Now in Smell-o-Vision!"

We laughed quietly, but the smell got stronger. I was starting to see a bit of haze in the air. This was like no special effect I'd ever seen. The planes droned by again, and I looked up to watch. Then I saw it: Flames were licking out the side of one of the planes. As I watched, one of the many tiny wires that held the plane up snapped from the heat, and the plane tilted crazily to one side! Flames were popping up all over.

"Joe!" I said, no longer trying to be quiet. "Look!"

The fiery prop plane was now belching out great clouds of smoke, flying over the audience and the stage in a big figure eight. No one else seemed to notice. Even just a ten-foot plane would kill someone if it landed on them! We had to do something before it came crashing to the stage—or worse!

I stood up, and another wire on the plane snapped! Now it was hanging entirely from one wing. And it was headed right toward the stage where Claire was singing!

"I'll go—"

"Save Claire!" I finished, already moving toward the fire extinguisher that glowed at the back of the theater. Joe took off running straight down the aisle.

I grabbed the extinguisher and ran out of the theater. In the lobby, I chose a door nearly at random. It was the one farthest to the side. If I was lucky, it would lead me to one of the box seats next to the stage.

I raced up the stairs, taking them three at a time. The fire extinguisher was cold and heavy in my hands. I just hoped I would be fast enough.

I burst through the curtains without a second to spare. The plane was passing right in front of me. I yanked the pin from the extinguisher, pointed the nozzle, and pulled the trigger. A cone of thick white stuff shot out from my hands like a fountain, blanketing the plane. I aimed for the remaining wires that held it up, but it was only within reach for a second, maybe two. Then it zoomed past me toward the stage. I dropped the extinguisher and ran to the edge of the booth.

The plane dripped foam as it flew directly at Claire. Because it was hanging from one wing, it was low enough to crack the skull of anyone in its path. Finally, other people in the theater had noticed. All action on the stage had stopped. Everyone was frozen in fear, except for that one dancer off in the corner, who was still doing her own thing. All the other actors stared in terror as the still smoldering wing of the plane zoomed right at Claire's head.

Suddenly, Joe came out of nowhere. He leapt onto the stage and landed in a roll, which took him directly to Claire. He reached her feet and bowled right over her, knocking her to the ground and safely out of the way.

"Phew," I let out a sigh of relief. That had been close. I peeled my fingers off the railing. My knuckles were white with fear. Talk about hitting the ground running.

Suddenly Joe called out from below.

"Nancy Drew? What are you doing here?!"

CHAPTER 4

JOE

COLD FEET

It took a second for me to come to my senses, what with the whole burning plane/fear of death thing. Struck dumb with surprise, I stared at the girl beneath me. The photos from ATAC hadn't done her justice. Aside from her dark hair, Claire Cleveland was a dead ringer for Nancy Drew!

"Are you going to help me up, or what?" said Claire, who had managed to turn "collapsed on the ground in a heap" into a model-like pose. All around us, the backup dancers were running around like chickens with their heads cut off, trying to get away from the dangling airplane above us. "Who's this Nancy girl? And who are you?"

"I'm Joe," I said. "Joe Hardy." I helped Claire to her feet. She smiled warmly at me.

"Jojo Hardy? What an interesting name." Claire stared directly into my eyes as she spoke, and I almost blushed.

"No, it's—it's Joe. Just Joe."

"Joe Just Joe?" Claire's eyes twinkled, and I realized she was teasing me. "You're cute. Nancy's a lucky girl."

"What? I mean . . . thank you. But no, she's not. I mean, she is, but she isn't my—"

"Is everyone okay?" Frank appeared at my side, which helped me pull my foot out of my mouth.

I nodded, still a little tongue-tied. All around us, people were hustling to lower the plane to the ground. Frank had put out the flames, and someone else had stopped it from moving, but it was still tons of metal dangling from a few tiny wires. I guided Nancy—I mean, Claire—offstage, as Frank moved to help two stagehands with the plane.

"Are you hurt?" I asked Claire.

She checked herself quickly. Up close, Claire looked young and sweet. But when I met her eyes, I could tell she was pretty tough. The whole incident didn't seem to have fazed her at all.

"I'm fine," she said with a smile. She patted her costume down. "But if I tore any of this, my dresser Jason is going to kill me."

She paused for a second, then shot me a cold look

that was a million miles away from the smiley, bubbly expression she'd just been wearing.

"You didn't answer my question," she said, edging back from me subtly. "Who are you?"

I didn't blame her for being suspicious. If I had that many crazy fans outside, I'd be nervous too. Nah, who am I kidding—if I had that many fans, I'd be out celebrating. But I understood where her fear was coming from. Most people weren't used to defying death on a daily basis. Luckily, it was one of my hobbies.

"Don't worry, we're your new bodyguards," I told Claire in a whisper.

Her smile returned. "Finally!" she said. "I told Linden if he didn't hire someone, I would—and he'd be paying either way. You're much cuter than the last bodyguards I had."

I was really starting to like this girl.

"You should be getting hazard pay for this," I joked.

The smile on Claire's face intensified. "Hazard pay? That's a brilliant idea. Excuse me, I have to call my agent."

Claire pulled a cell phone from her pocket and stepped farther into the wings.

I heard a man groan from the other side of the stage. "Great! Looks like we'll be renegotiating her contract. Again. And we have to replace another plane! Damien! Where are you?"

A tall blond man strode toward me. He was suave and well dressed. I'd noticed him from the corner of my eye as I'd run to the stage. He looked exactly like the photo ATAC had showed us.

"Linden von Louden," he said, grabbing my hand in a manly shake. "The producer of this . . ." he paused for a minute, as if trying to decide what to call it. "Show," he finished eventually.

"Joe Hardy," I said. I was about to mention my cover story—that Frank and I were aspiring high school students who wanted to work on Broadway shows, and we'd won a competition to watch Wake develop in its last week. Often, our local contacts couldn't remember who we were supposed to be, even when they'd invented the cover story. I didn't want him to slip up and identify us as members of ATAC in front of all these people.

"Ah, our contest winners! We've been waiting for you," Linden responded smoothly. Looked as if Claire wasn't the only decent actor on this stage. I was impressed. He leaned in toward me. "You look just like the headshots—I mean photos—ATAC sent over. If you ever get tired of undercover work, give me a call. I know a role that'd be perfect for you." He slipped a business card into my hand.

"Uh, thanks?" I was a little taken aback. I mean, my model good looks are pretty stunning, but didn't you need to be able to act to get on Broadway? "That's my brother, Frank." I pointed over to the tight huddle of techie types who were gathered around the plane.

"And that's my sister, Laurel," Linden jerked his thumb back behind him. Half hidden in one of the curtains was a striking blond woman in a gold dress, tapping away at the screen of her smartphone.

"She'll be with us as soon as she finishes tweeting," Linden continued. "So, maybe an hour or two, right Laurel?"

Laurel was silent for a few seconds as she continued to type. Then she lifted her head. "I'm sorry," she said. "I was busy making sure the press release went out for tonight. You know, just trying to save our show. Was I inconveniencing you?"

"Not more than usual," Linden responded with a smile. Laurel snorted.

If there's one thing I know well, it's siblings who work together. It was obvious that Laurel and Linden loved each other just slightly more than they hated each other.

Laurel's handshake was just as firm as her brother's. "Laurel," she said.

"Joe," I responded. "And this is my brother, Frank."

"Good to meet you," said Frank.

"So what's the story with the plane?" I asked him.

"I can't tell. It looks like the engine shorted, but

whether it was an accident or on purpose, I won't be able to tell without a closer look. Can we put it somewhere where I can examine it later?"

Linden nodded. Side-by-side, Laurel and Linden looked amazingly alike. Same hair, same height, same eyes. Linden was more outgoing and friendly, but aside from that, they were a matched set.

"But make sure you don't mess it up," said Laurel. She paused. "I mean, any more than it already is. It could have some resale value."

"Excuse me! Sorry! Mr. von Louden? You wanted me?"

A short man approached. His hair was black and his skin was very pale. He looked even younger than Frank and I, but from the headset he wore and the clipboard he carried, it was obvious he worked here.

"Oh, look," said Laurel. "It's your pet."

The guy blushed a brilliant red and stared down at his shoes.

Linden snapped his fingers.

"Damien!" he said. Somehow he managed to have all the intensity of a full scream without going above a normal speaking voice. "How many times have I told you to stay with me at all times?"

"Yes sir, I know. It's just . . . you . . . you . . . asked me to go—" Damien stammered his way through an answer, but Linden wasn't listening.

"This is Joe and Frank Hardy. They won that contest I told you about, remember?"

Damien nodded.

"They can go anywhere they want, ask any questions, talk to anyone. If they need anything, you'll help them out. And tomorrow, you'll give them a tour of the entire backstage area."

Damien scribbled frantically on his clipboard while Linden spoke. "Tour, tomorrow. Got it. Anything else?"

"There's a preview in thirty minutes. Find these guys good seats, and do something about the missing plane."

Something, Damien scribbled on his pad, and I had to pity the poor guy. That didn't look like a fun job.

"You're going to have a show, now?" I asked, shocked. A flaming plane had nearly crashed into the stage—and Claire!

"Gentlemen," Linden smiled big. "This is Broadway. PLACES!"

Linden clapped his hands and everyone started scrambling.

"If you two could, uh, follow me?" Damien said. He led us back into the wing, near where Claire had gone.

"So what do you do here?" I asked, trying to play our cover story.

"I'm Linden's assistant," he said. "So I do a little of everything."

It was hard to imagine Damien having a full-time

job of any kind, let alone working for someone as high-powered as Linden von Louden. But he must have had some kinds of skills, because Linden didn't seem like the type to put up with incompetence. In fact, our briefing had mentioned Linden's short temper as one of his dominant characteristics.

Damien pulled two folding chairs out from behind a giant piece of scenery and put them just offstage, almost in view of the audience.

"This mark is the sight line from the front row," he said, pointing to a thin piece of tape on the ground. "Whatever you do, don't go past it. In fact, don't get out of these chairs—actors are going to be running on and off right past you, and if you get in their way, it'll throw the whole scene off."

With that, he disappeared, leaving Frank and me alone. Or well, as alone as we could be considering that fifty people were rushing around us, getting ready for the preview.

"So this is like . . . a pre-opening show? Is it a dress rehearsal?"

"No," said Frank. "It's a chance for people to see the full show, so that Linden can gauge their reaction and see if there's anything that needs to be changed."

"Judging by what we saw earlier, I'd say pretty much everything needs to change, except for Claire! What's your read on the plane?"

"It could have been an accident . . . but I doubt it. The real question is, who sabotaged it and how?"

I was about to respond, when Claire swept over to us. She was dressed for the preview in a period WWII uniform. A wig had been put over her real hair, giving her long curly brown locks that made her look like less of a teenager, and more of a pinup star.

She laid her hand on Frank's shoulder.

"So, what exactly are your bodyguard duties?" she asked.

Frank blushed, and I almost snorted. I loved watching girls hit on Frank. He never knew how to handle it, even with a girl like Claire who clearly flirted with everyone.

"Well, we, you know, we look after you and make sure you're safe."

"If I was in danger, you'd do something?" she asked, leaning in closer.

"Of course!" Frank blurted out.

"Well," said Claire with a big smile. "Right now, I'm in danger of dying of thirst. Would you be a dear and get a juice pack from my dressing room? They're in the fridge."

Frank smiled ruefully. He'd walked right into that one.

"Sure thing, Claire," he said gracefully. Once he was gone, she flopped down in his chair.

"You seem pretty calm about this whole near-death-experience thing," I said, hoping to get to know her a little better. She seemed nice, but she barely seemed to care about the threats and the accidents. I hated to suspect our client, but we'd seen this sort of thing before, people faking danger for attention.

Claire laughed. "I've been on television since I was three. I got my first marriage proposal at seven, and my first death threat when I was ten. Two years ago, some girl got plastic surgery to look like me and managed to steal my yacht. Which we still haven't recovered. So yeah, I'm pretty calm about this. It's all part of being famous."

I smiled. There was more to Claire than met the eye.

"How's it looking out there?" she asked. I leaned forward in my chair, past Damien's tape mark.

"Well . . ."

"Empty, huh?" she said.

"Not completely, but yeah."

"That's what I figured. Still, a star must go on. Thank you."

Frank reappeared and handed her a juice box. She sucked it down in one quick gulp. She made no effort to get up from his chair. Damien scurried around us like an ant, doing this job and then the next. In fact, everyone except for Claire seemed to be in a complete panic. The energy backstage was so intense you could feel it—as opposed to the energy in the front of the house, which was pretty much nonexistent.

"I don't get it," said Frank. "How can you have such an army of fans outside, but no one at the show?"

"Those fans?" said Claire with a yawn. "Those are *my* fans. They're not here for the show. They're here for me. Besides, they've all read the blogs. This show is falling apart."

She grimaced.

"That bad, huh?" I asked.

"No," she said, rubbing her stomach. "I mean, yes, it is. But actually, right now, I don't feel so well."

A shiver ran through her.

"Places!" Linden yelled from the other side of the stage. "On in five!"

"Ms. Cleveland?" said Damien, in a voice so quiet I could barely hear him. "Are you okay?"

Claire had turned seriously green. Something was wrong. She stood up.

"I'm going to be sick. Oh no!"

She clapped a hand over her mouth and ran toward the bathroom. Damien looked as if he were going to cry.

"No! Ms. Cleveland, come back!"

"What is the problem here? Damien! Where is my star?" Linden appeared, his face an angry red.

"Mr. von Louden, she's sick. She just ran to the

bathroom. Should I go see what's wrong?" Damien wrung his hands in worry.

"There's no time. Get Madonna in costume and put her on the stage. We're live in three minutes. I thought Claire was never sick!"

The last part was yelled generally at the stage crew as Linden stalked off. Damien ran off, his face set in a terrified expression.

Gone was the suave, cool, and collected Linden we'd met earlier. Now he was raging backstage, exactly like everyone I'd ever seen play a director in the movies. Or a crazy person. Was it just preshow jitters? Or did someone have an anger management problem?

"I'll check on Claire," volunteered Frank.

"I'll keep an eye on things here," I said, throwing one leg up on his chair. I was definitely enjoying this mission.

A young girl raced by wearing Claire's costume. As the orchestra played the opening notes, Damien handed the girl a wig and she took her place in the wings. I recognized her from our ATAC briefing. She was Madonna de la Varga, Claire's understudy.

"This is unheard of," whispered Damien under his breath. "Wow!"

"What is?" said Frank, sliding back into his chair. To me, he whispered "Stomach bug. She seems fine."

"Claire has only missed one show in her entire life, an afternoon matinee when she was nine. She broke her arm, but she was back in time for the evening show. There's a mini-documentary about it on YouTube." Damien paused for a second. "I made it," he whispered with pride.

The tone in Damien's voice indicated an emotion I'd witnessed on a dozen cases before: obsession. The hair on the back of my neck rose. I looked at Frank, and he nodded. He'd noticed it too. We'd definitely be keeping an eye on this guy.

Madonna stepped out onto the stage, and the applause began. Damien scurried off to work on something, and Frank and I sat back to enjoy the show.

Or I should say, endure the show. Without Claire, the performance had as much sparkle and fun as a chunk of concrete. The dancers limped around the stage. Madonna forgot her lines twice. Whatever they'd done to get the burned plane down had disabled the other two, leaving them hanging motionless over the audience for the entire show.

It was so painful that it was a relief when Madonna readied for the last number before the intermission. This was her big emotional ballad, and as she stepped into the spotlight she raised her hands up in the air and prepared to make the most of it.

Then she opened her mouth, stepped forward—and fell right through a hole in the stage!

MOBBED!

"Okay, tell me what they told you again?" Bess asked.

She popped her gum and slumped back in her seat, a jittery expression on her face. Next to her, George tapped away on her phone. We'd been stuck in traffic for forty minutes now, and if we didn't get off the West Side Highway soon, one of us was going to lose it.

"Apparently, they're working on a new case that involves this show on Broadway called *Wake*. The lead actress, Claire Cleveland, has been receiving death threats. Two days ago her understudy broke her leg in an accident that Joe says was almost certainly meant for Claire."

"Claire Cleveland," said Bess, her voice dreamy. "I love her TV show!" She launched into the chorus of the theme song, and the man in the car next to us made a big show of rolling up his windows. Bess had many talents, but singing wasn't one of them.

"So they want you to be her understudy?" said George loudly, trying to talk over Bess.

"Yes. But they've promised me I won't have to go onstage. Apparently, Claire is known for never missing a show."

"Except for the other night," George teased.

I was trying not to think about that. I could imagine a few things worse than having to sing on a Broadway stage—but they all involved tarring and feathering.

"They think she was poisoned! It wasn't her fault. And with me as her understudy, nothing is going to pass through her lips unless I've checked it first."

"I told you that you looked like Claire Cleveland!" said Bess, hitting the steering wheel with her hand. "See, it would have been the perfect Halloween outfit last year. All you needed was a wig."

As suddenly as it had stopped, traffic started moving again. We were over on the west side of Manhattan, making our way down along the Hudson River. To the right, the view of the parks and the river was so pretty that you'd never know you were in New York City—until you turned your head in the other direction, and saw the dozens upon dozens of skyscrapers clawing up at the sky. There were a lot of people in this city, and at least one of them wanted to hurt, or possibly kill, a girl who looked like my twin.

Just great, I thought. Still, I had to admit I was excited. I guess that was why I became a private detective in the first place.

Finally, Forty-third Street appeared on our left. I looked at my watch. I was only . . . twenty minutes late.

"That's it up ahead," said George, pointing to an elegant marble façade. The words "Wake—Starring Claire Cleveland!" were picked out in neon across the marquee. A large crowd of people had gathered in front of the theater. They had to be waiting for tonight's show.

"Nancy, why don't you get out here and we'll find somewhere to park?" Bess offered, and I agreed, eager to hit the ground running on this case. Besides, I couldn't think of anything less fun than circling Manhattan looking for a parking space.

"You're the best!" I yelled, as I hopped out of the car. The delicious smell of roasted nuts wafted from a vendor's cart, and for a second, I was tempted to be even later than I was. But my need for clues was stronger than my need for sweets.

As Bess and George drove away, I crossed the street toward the crowd waiting for the show. They were mostly people around my own age, although I saw some kids who barely came up to my waist, and a few older folks as well. As I got closer, I could see that many of them were holding pictures of Claire, or *Playbill*s from the show. I guess they were waiting to see it for a second time. As I pushed through the back edge of the crowd, I stared at one of the photos. Bess was right. Claire and I looked a lot alike.

"Excuse me!" I said, worming my way through a moving wall of arms and legs and backpacks. "I'm late, please let me through."

"Oh, wow!" A girl about my age grabbed my hand as I tried to move past her. She was taller than I was, and surprisingly strong. "It's her! I'm touching her."

Clearly, she had mistaken me for Claire. I was about to explain, when she turned to the rest of the crowd and screamed.

"She's here! Claire Cleveland is here, and I'm holding her hand!"

The entire crowd turned to face us. People started whispering and pointing, then screaming and shoving. Suddenly, I realized I was alone and completely cut off from any escape route.

"No, no!" I said, trying to shake the girl off. If I could just get loose, I might make a run for the theater. But she had me in a death grip. "I'm sorry, there's been some confusion. I'm not Claire Cleveland. My name is Nancy. Nancy Drew!"

No one listened. People were pushing in, crowding around us, grabbing at me. Some were thrusting pens and pictures in my face, while others were taking photos with their cell phones. The space around me was getting smaller and smaller, until people were pressed up against me on every side! I could barely breathe. The excited shrieks of the crowd were like the hungry cries of a flock of birds, and I was beginning to understand how worms felt.

"Ow!" I screamed. Someone had yanked a piece of my hair out! This had gone too far. I pushed—and the crowd pushed back! I fell to my side, but there was nowhere to go. Someone shoved me from behind, and I stumbled face first into a woman's giant backpack. The yelling of the crowd had turned from excited and happy to scared and angry.

"Calm down, everyone!" I yelled. "Please, stop this!"

"I can't breathe!"

"Someone took my wallet!"

"Help!"

Everyone was panicking. In ten seconds, the scene on the sidewalk had turned into a riot—and I was right at the center of it.

Someone new grabbed my hand, hard. I yanked my arm back, but they hung on. I felt myself slowly being dragged out of the crowd. I didn't know who it was, but if there was a way out, I was going to follow. As gently as I could, I pushed my way forward.

"I'm sorry," I said over and over again. But everyone was pushing, and there was nothing else I could do.

"Help!" yelled a small voice below me. I looked down and saw a young girl, maybe twelve, lying on the ground. Feet were stomping all around her. It was only a matter of time before she was trampled.

I reached down and pulled her to her feet.

"Amy! Amy, oh God, there you are!" a woman yelled. The girl grabbed her mother's arm, and my mysterious benefactor pulled us away.

"Mommy! Claire Cleveland saved my life!" I heard, as we swept away through the crowd. I couldn't help but smile. Even if I did nothing else, I'd at least managed to give Claire a good reputation.

Finally I found myself pulled up against a metal fence. It was nice to only have people pushing at me from one side—and even nicer when part of the fence swung open, and I was yanked into a small alleyway next to the theater. It was blissfully empty and quiet.

"Thank you. I don't know what I would have done if you hadn't arrived when you did," I said, getting a close look at my savior for the first time. Up close, he was shorter than I was, and cute, in a leprechaun kind of way. He had curly dark hair and flawless pale skin. He looked like he worked at the theater. At least, he wore a headset and held a clipboard. If he didn't work at the theater, he had strange fashion sense.

He puffed his hair out of his eyes, causing his curls to flop around.

"Sorry about that," he said. He seemed genuinely sorry, as though the mob's panic had been his fault. He wouldn't meet my eyes. He was even blushing a little.

"It's okay," I said. "I'm Nancy."

"Nancy Drew," he responded. "I know. You're on my list." He pointed to his clipboard. "I'm Damien Alexander. Assistant to Mr. Linden von Louden."

"Good to meet you, Damien," I shook his hand, then tried to rearrange my hair into something that didn't look like a bird's nest. "I think the crowd mistook me for Claire and got . . . excited."

Excited was the most charitable way I could put it. Wild might have been more appropriate, or maybe insane.

"I know!" he said, suddenly looking up. His eyes, I noticed, had a bit of a wild flair to them, like a gypsy in a movie. "It's ridiculous, because you two look nothing alike. Claire is at least three-quarters of an inch taller than you, and her hair is so much darker. I guess there's a little resemblance in the face, but Claire is the most beautiful woman in showbiz. No offense."

He snapped his mouth shut. His sudden rant about Claire seemed to have surprised Damien as much as it did me. Okay . . . there was something a little off about this guy. I'd have to talk to Frank and Joe about him. Which reminded me . . .

"I, uh, am late for a meeting," I started, not wanting to seem rude or ungrateful. Damien blushed instantly.

"Right! Yes, sorry. Go through that door there," he said, pointing to a red fire door farther down the alley. "Take a left when you get inside. They're waiting for you. I have to go calm that mob scene down and let the people with tickets in. Wish me luck!"

With that, Damien disappeared back out to the sidewalk, quickly closing and locking the gate behind him.

I paused as I stepped through the door into the darkness beyond. This would be my first time backstage at a Broadway musical! Even the crazy crowd couldn't take away my excitement. How many famous people had stepped through this door before me?

The backstage area was bustling as I walked in. The scenery was laid out in sections for the different acts. It all sat on tracks in the floor, or hung from ropes, so it could be pulled on or off quickly. There were costumes and clothes and props everywhere. A half-dozen people, dressed all in black and wearing headsets, scurried around making sure everything was ready to go.

"Nancy!" Frank Hardy yelled my name from across the way. "There you are."

CHAPTER **6**

F R A N K

TRAPPED!

After Nancy arrived, we quickly introduced her to Claire, Linden, and Laurel. While Claire prepared for the night's show, we brought Nancy up to speed. It was great having her on the case with us. We'd worked together many times in the past, and Nancy Drew was just about the best partner we'd ever found. We'd tried repeatedly to get her to join ATAC, but she'd said it wasn't her thing.

By the time Bess and George joined us, the show was about to start. Together, we watched from the wings as Claire got ready to perform before a preview audience ten times the size of the one from the night before.

"This is incredible," said Nancy. "There are so many

people here. Everything I read online said the show wasn't doing well."

"It's not—you'll see in a second," I told her. Unless the show had magically improved, this big audience was in for a big disappointment.

"It's the injury," said Joe. "Word was all around the Internet before Madonna had even made it to the hospital. Ticket sales spiked immediately. They're saying the show is haunted!"

"Haunted?" Nancy laughed. "Every haunting I've ever dealt with has been decidedly nonsupernatural in origin. Any leads?"

"None yet, but now that you're here, we're hoping that'll change quickly."

"So what's the plan?" Nancy asked.

"You're taking the place of Madonna, Claire's understudy, so you'll have a reason to be stuck like glue to her for the next few days. While you're doing that, we're going to look into some of the strange things that have happened here in the last week."

The lights dimmed, and the music rose. Bess grabbed my hand in excitement.

"Let's all meet here tomorrow at nine," I whispered, as the show began.

When we arrived the next morning, Claire, Linden, and Nancy were already in one of the rehearsal rooms. It was a great relief to know that Nancy was looking after Claire. I almost felt bad for whoever was "haunting" the theater. Almost.

Damien was waiting in the lobby to give us a tour, as Linden had promised. We'd hoped to do it yesterday, but before Nancy arrived, we'd been too worried to let Claire out of our sight.

"Good morning boys," Damien said. Now that he knew we were "high school contest winners," he talked to us as though we were infants. "Are you ready for your tour?"

I nodded. It was best to get this over with fast. At least it would cement our cover story in everyone's minds.

"This is the lobby of the Matilda Swearson Theatre, which was originally built in 1908 by the Swearson family. Of particular interest are the columns."

Damien paused and pointed to the nine columns around the room. Each had a woman carved into the marble.

"These represent the nine muses: Calliope, Clio, Erato, Euterpe, Melpomene, Polyhymnia, Terpsichore, Thalia, and Urania. You'll notice the four central ones are bigger. That's because respectively, Melpomene, Terpsichore, Euterpe, and Thalia represent tragedy, dance, music, and comedy. Together, they make a Broadway show. Now, the mosaic above our heads . . ."

Joe nudged me and rolled his eyes. "Boring!" he mouthed.

For once, I had to agree. I'm all for learning anything, anywhere, because you never know what might come in handy. But Damien lectured like a half-asleep kindergarten teacher.

Slowly, he led us through the lobby, up into the mezzanine, back down into the orchestra, and all through the "front of the house." That was how he referred to all of the areas that theatergoers were generally allowed into. Then, he took us backstage. It was surprising to learn how much had to happen to make a show run. There were as many people backstage as there were onstage, maybe even more. There were tiny rooms and hidden staircases, two levels of basement storage, and "the grid"—a giant set of walkways above the entire stage and audience. The grid was where things like the lights and planes hung from. I made a mental note to check it out later.

Damien's knowledge of the theater bordered on obsessive, but I guess that's what made him good at his job. When we reached the stage, I had to interrupt his monologue.

"Where's the hole that Madonna fell through?"

"The *trap*," Damien corrected me, "is over there." He pointed to center of the stage. "I checked it myself. It's fine. Someone must have left it unlatched. In the second act, Claire is supposed to rise up from it when she escapes from her secret hiding hole in Nazi-occupied Paris."

"Who would touch this?" I asked.

"Myself, the technical director, any number of production assistants . . . really, it could have been anyone. But no one should have opened it that early. It might have just given way under Madonna's weight. She has seven pounds on Claire."

I shot Joe a look. That was an odd fact to know, and it seemed unlikely that seven pounds would be enough to break the trap door. I filed it away for later. Nothing seemed wrong with the trap, at least not at first glance.

"I fixed the latch this morning," Damien said proudly.

No wonder there's no evidence, I thought.

A laugh rang out on the other side of the theater.

"I love this girl," yelled Claire. She flounced out of the rehearsal room dragging Nancy behind her. They were wearing matching WWII uniforms. Nancy looked a little embarrassed, but she was smiling. It was obvious things were going well between them.

"Joe! Frank! Come here," yelled Claire. "You have to hear what Nancy just told me."

Claire threw one arm over my shoulders and another over Joe's. In general, girls make me kind of nervous. But Claire was the kind of person who made everyone feel like her best friend. I glanced over my shoulder as

Nancy told us a story about her last case. Damien was staring at us with unconcealed jealousy.

"Where's Linden?" I asked. "Wasn't he with you?"

"Yeah," said Claire. "But he and Laurel are having their daily fight now."

She shrugged, making it clear it was nothing she cared about.

"So Joe, you wanted to talk to me?" Claire grinned, kissed me on the cheek, and pulled Joe aside, leaving Nancy and me alone.

"How's it going?" I asked.

"Good. Learning a show is a crazy workout!" she said. "But what are you doing with that creepy kid Damien?"

My ears perked up. If Nancy thought he was creepy, that meant it wasn't just my imagination.

"He's Linden's assistant, I guess, though he seems a little young."

"A little young and a little stalker-y! Remember I told you about that guy who rescued me from the crowd yesterday, and how he knew all these odd facts about Claire?"

"Uh-huh," I nodded. I was pretty sure I knew where this was going.

"That's him!"

"I'll keep an eye on him today," I promised. "He's got my danger-senses tingling too."

But when I turned around, Damien had disappeared. Nancy rejoined Claire and Joe, and I was left alone onstage.

"So much for the rest of that tour," I mumbled. Not that I minded, really. But I did want to keep Damien close. I had other concerns this morning, though. Since Claire seemed safe with Joe and Nancy, I headed down to the subbasement. There was a small room of broken props down there: things from old shows that might be reusable, as well as pieces from this show in need of repair. Laurel had moved the burned plane down there to see what could be rescued, but she'd promised me first crack at it.

The first basement level was where the wardrobe people worked. They made the costumes, fixed any damage that happened during the performances, and helped the actors get into and out of their clothes between scenes. Three or four people were gathered around sewing machines and bins of period hats and shoes. Jason, Claire's dresser, waved to me. He had bright pink hair and a quick smile. Claire said that without him, she'd lose her head—literally.

Past the wardrobe area was an old metal staircase that led to the lowest level of the theater. I stepped onto the stair and closed the heavy fire door behind me, instantly cutting off any noise from above. Because there were so many people working backstage, all of the different areas were as soundproof as possible. This kept the audience from hearing strange noises during the show. I tried not to worry about what else we might not be able to hear.

Props were laid out on long rows of shelves. The biggest pieces, like a giant clown head with bright pink eyes, leaned against the back wall. It was a quiet, creepy place. I didn't want to spend any more time here than I had to.

"Anyone in here?" I called out as I entered the repair shop. Something skittered behind me, but unless Claire was being stalked by a mouse, I didn't think it was anything to worry about.

The room was filled to the brim with tools, art supplies, and broken props. The plane was laid out in the center of the room on a heavy wooden table. Most of the paint had burned off, and what remained was flaky and discolored. It really did look as if it had been through a war. Maybe they could find a use for it if they ever did a sequel to this show, but its life as a working airplane seemed over to me.

I pulled a small kit from my pocket. A casual observer would think it was a glasses case, but it was actually a mini-forensics kit that Vijay had invented. With this, I could dust for fingerprints, check for bloodstains, and send chemical samples back to ATAC wirelessly.

"Darn," I said, as I put fingerprint powder all over the

plane. As I'd suspected, nothing useful had survived the fire. As gently as I could, I opened the panel to reveal the engine. The hinges groaned and then snapped.

"Oops," I muttered, as I was left holding the panel in my hands. I tried to put it aside, but one of my fingers was stuck to the inside.

"Eww!"

Whatever the stuff was, it was so sticky it nearly pulled my skin off! Intrigued, I removed what looked like a plastic Q-tip from my kit. Vijay had built it to analyze the chemical structure of any compound. It sent the information back to him in his lab, where he could synthesize it and figure out what it was. I dabbed the plastic head in the sticky resin, pulling back almost as soon as I touched the stuff. I didn't want to end up with my sensor permanently stuck to the engine block.

I peered inside the engine compartment. The worst of the damage was in here. All I saw was dust, scorch marks, and blackened metal. After a minute of poking, I knew I'd learn nothing. If this was sabotage, the person had done a good job of covering their tracks.

A booming sound came from outside the repair room.

"Hello?" I yelled. My voice echoed back at me. "Is anyone out there?"

No one responded. I grabbed a wrench from among the tools on the table, and slowly crept back out into the main room. Everything looked exactly as it had a few minutes before.

A shiver shot down my spine. This place was creeping me out, and I'd learned what I could from the plane. It was time to get out of here.

"I could have sworn this door opened out," I said, as I pushed against the heavy fire door. I tried pulling on it, but to no avail. I grabbed the handle and rattled it as hard as I could, but the door stayed stubbornly in place.

I ducked my head down and prepared to give the door a good shoulder slam, but something caught my eye: a plain white sheet of paper on the ground. In big penciled letters, someone had written "LEAVE!"

Just in case I didn't get the message, they'd underlined it. Twice.

Too bad for them I wasn't good at taking hints.

"Hey!" I yelled, as I pounded on the door. "Let me out!"

The heavy metal door absorbed the sound, and all I got for the effort was a sore hand. *This could take a while*, I realized.

After fifteen minutes of calling for help, my throat started to get sore. After thirty, I could feel a bruise forming on my right hand, so I switched to hitting the door with my left.

Finally, after nearly an hour, the door cracked open to reveal Bess, George, and Claire's dresser, Jason.

"Woohoo!" I whooped. "I've been pounding on that door forever."

"What are you doing down here?" George asked. "Jason was showing us around. If he hadn't opened the door, we'd have never heard you on the other side."

"Long story," I said, hiding the piece of paper behind my back so Jason wouldn't see it. You could never be too careful.

CHAPTER 7

JOE

MY CUP RUNNETH OVER . . . WITH POISON!

I can't lie: I was excited to get off of Damien's magical memorization tour. That guy knew more useless facts than Frank, and Frank studied trivia like it was his job! (And, okay, sometimes it comes in handy on a case, so I guess it *is* his job.) When Claire pulled me aside, I jumped on the chance to escape. We walked over to a quiet corner behind a giant piece of scenery meant to evoke Paris during the war.

"So what's up?" Claire asked, twirling her hair around her finger and leaning against a painted lamp post. "Nancy says you have a few questions for me?"

I smiled big at Claire and got ready to work my patented "mo-Joe" on her.

"I wanted to ask you about the other night. What happened that made you miss the show?"

"You were there," she said with a smirk. "You know what happened."

My mo-Joe must have been off. I tried again.

"Yeah, but . . . what happened? Tell me like I wasn't there."

"I got sick, okay?" Claire huffed. This was clearly a subject that made her irritated. "It sucks. I'm *never* sick. I can't let down my fans like that."

I was pretty sure the juice box was our culprit, but I needed to make sure she hadn't eaten anything else.

"When did you start feeling sick?"

"Right before we went on. I was talking to you, and I had my juice, and then my stomach started to cramp real bad. The next thing I knew, I was saying hi to my lunch."

"Where do the juice boxes come from?"

"They're in my rider. I require them on every set. Meredith used to stock them for me, but since she quit . . . I don't know who's been doing it."

"Meredith?"

"My personal assistant. She quit two weeks ago."

A recently departed employee? Someone who must have been super close to Claire? I smelled a suspect! Maybe the poisoned juice box was some sort of twisted good-bye present.

"Really? How did you two get along? Where did she go?"

"She was the worst!" said Claire with an exaggerated sigh. "She didn't cut me any slack. Once, she dragged me out of bed for a meeting. I mean, literally dragged me. I'm a star! I don't take that."

This was sounding better and better. The case was going to be wrapped up by lunch.

"Of course, that's why I loved her. I can't have a bunch of yes-men around letting me do whatever I want, or I'd never do anything. Meredith was perfect. Too bad she moved to Russia."

Aaaaand there went that suspect. My disappointment must have shown on my face, because Claire reached out and brushed the hair back from my forehead.

"Poor bodyguard!" she said. "I can promise you, Meredith would never do anything like that. I mean, she left me for the prima ballerina at the Bolshoi Ballet—she's not that kind of girl."

"Thanks." I couldn't help but smile. "Can I get the key to your dressing room? I want to check out the remaining juices."

"Claire! Nancy!" Linden yelled from the other room. "Break's over."

"No rest for the weary," Claire says. "Though, since we open tomorrow, I *guess* it makes sense."

Claire handed me the key and flounced off, with Nancy trailing behind her. Frank looked at me and tossed his head in the direction of the heavy iron door that led to the basement levels. He must have been going to investigate the plane. I headed over to Claire's dressing room. We'd already sent the used juice box container to Vijay to analyze its contents, but I was hoping our poisoner might have left something behind.

The dressing rooms were all upstairs from the stage, sort of like where the mezzanine was in the audience. As the star, Claire had her own. It was easy to find. It was the only door with a giant cutout of Claire on it.

Inside, the room was actually rather simple. There were a few flowers, a *New York Times* article praising Claire's performance on *Joy!*, a wooden dressing table, a few chairs, and a small fridge. Everything—including the fridge—was pink. Claire promised that no one had touched the fridge since Frank got her juice box, but just to be sure, I'd placed a tiny piece of clear tape on the bottom of the door, right after she'd gotten sick.

"Yes!" I said, as I ran my hand underneath the fridge. The tape was still there in one piece. The evidence was undisturbed.

The fridge was filled with lots of bright green coconut water juice boxes—and nothing else. There must have been thirty identical containers. This was going to take a while.

Just then, my phone rang. I looked at the screen—Vijay!

"Hey man," I said. "Tell me you have some news for me."

"What, you think I'm calling just to talk to you? Not." Vijay laughed. "That juice box you sent me? Definitely dosed, my friend. But here's the weird part: It had ipecac in it."

"Ipecac?" I asked. "Isn't that medicine?"

"Yes and no. It's an emetic, which means it'll make you puke. But lots of people have it in their medicine cabinet. You said Claire's been receiving death threats?"

"Yeah, and the other night someone nearly killed her understudy."

"Ipecac wouldn't kill anyone. They give it to children all the time. The worst it can do is ruin your evening."

Hmm . . . that was interesting news, even if I didn't know how it fit in with the rest of the case. Yet.

"Hey Veej, can you do me a favor?" I asked, pulling my portable forensic kit out.

"No, I cannot get you the new ZOMG Kill game."

"Not that! If I sample these juice boxes right now, can you tell if they all have ipecac in them?"

"Sure, now that I know what I'm looking for I can do that in a few seconds."

One by one, we tested the juices. Each one came up

positive for ipecac. Someone wanted to make certain Claire didn't go on last night.

"How hard would it have been for someone to do this?" I asked Vijay.

"Easy-peasy, my friend. With a syringe and a bottle of ipecac, this could be done in . . . five minutes maybe?"

The boxes came up negative for everything else: no fingerprints, no other poisons, no identifying marks.

"Oprah's back on," Vijay said. "I have to go."

"Oprah?" I started to ask, but the line was already dead. Veej was a weird dude, but I liked him.

All right, Joe, I told myself. *Think.*

This wasn't a coincidence. These drinks didn't come pre-poisoned. So all I needed to do was follow what the cops called the "chain of evidence." If I could make a list of everyone who touched these juice boxes since they entered the theater, the poisoner would have to be on it. I needed to talk to someone in charge.

I locked the dressing room behind me. A flash of pink hair appeared out of the corner of my eye and I saw Jason, Claire's dresser, walking by carrying a poorly balanced stack of women's shoes.

"Sorry, coming through," he said as he passed. The top pair of shoes slipped off his stack, and I hurried to pick them up.

"Thanks," he said, as I placed them on top of the pile. "I've got to get all of these polished by tonight!"

"That's a lot of work!" I said. An idea occurred to me. "Hey, maybe you can help me with something. When we do our shows back home, we don't have a lot of staff. How do you guys handle it when someone leaves unexpectedly? Like, when Meredith left, who took over her job?"

"Oh, man," said Jason. "Usually, I'm the one who has to take up the slack. But it wasn't me when Meredith left. . . ." He thought for a second.

"Honestly, I don't know," he said finally. "Maybe ask Laurel? Someone had to be paid to do it, and if there's any money involved, Laurel is in the middle of it."

"Thanks," I yelled as Jason rushed off. "Do you know where I could find her?"

"Her office! Top floor."

Although Laurel was one of the hottest producers on Broadway, her office was smaller than I had expected. It had a faded green carpet and a wooden desk that, although elegant, had seen better days. The two giant computer screens on top of it, however, were top of the line.

"Yes?" Laurel said as I walked in. Her fingers were flying across her keyboard, and she only pulled her eyes away from the screens for half a second to see who I was.

"I had a question for you. Do you have a minute?" I asked, trying to be polite—she was our employer.

"Sure," she said.

Laurel didn't even pause her typing, so I leapt right in.

"I have a question about Claire's juice boxes."

"Rider seven point two in her contract. Costs us about thirty-five dollars per week. It's the price of having a star. Just one of those adorable little perks."

The way she said the word "adorable" made it sound like a four-letter word.

"That wasn't my question actually. I was wondering if you knew who got them for her."

"Purchasing is my department. I order them through Whole Foods."

She still wasn't getting it. All she seemed to care about was the money, not the fact that the juices had been poisoned. I needed to get her attention. I put my hand on top of her computer monitor. Suddenly, she had eyes for nothing but me.

"I mean, who brings them to her?" I asked, trying to be as clear as possible.

Laurel looked at me coldly.

"I'm sorry. I didn't realize that on top of funding this show, running the house, and writing your paycheck, I had to know who is responsible for *bringing Claire a juice box*."

I took my hand off the monitor.

"I'll ask someone else," I said, but she'd already turned back to her computer.

As I reached the main floor of the theater, I ran into Damien coming up the stairs.

Maybe, I thought, *this might be something Mr. Encyclopedia here could help me with.*

I used the same lie I'd told Jason, asking who did what tasks around the theater.

"Claire's juices?" Damien said. "Originally it was Meredith who got them for her. But when she left Madonna took over. Then Madonna threw a fit three days ago, and I started stocking the fridge."

"So you put the juices in the fridge the night Claire got sick?"

Damien shook his head. "No, I put them in the day before. But I don't think anyone else would have touched them."

Jackpot!

I smiled, and Damien tilted his head and looked at me sideways for a second. A thoughtful expression crossed his face.

"Say," he said. "Where did you say you were from again?"

"Bayport," I answered. "Frank and I work with the Bayport Regional Theater."

"Interesting," said Damien. "I've never heard of that theater. Are you guys Equity? Union?"

Thankfully, all of this had been covered in our briefing.

"Not yet." I shook my head as though I were terribly

sad about it. "Frank and I are hoping that we can learn enough here this week to really bring the theater to the next level."

"So what shows have you done?"

"Uhh . . . *Bye Bye Birdie*, *The Music Man*, you know, the usual."

This conversation was starting to go dangerous places. I tried to edge past Damien on the stairs, but he threw his arm out and leaned against the wall, blocking my exit.

"So you guys are big Sondheim fans?" He smiled. "Me too."

"We love him," I nodded. "Now, if you don't mind, I have to—"

"That's funny," said Damien. "Because none of those shows are by Sondheim."

He'd caught me. There was only one way out of this. I needed to bluff, and bluff hard.

"Look, I don't have time for this," I said, trying my best to act calmer than I felt. Our cover was in danger of being blown. "I'm not here to explain myself to you. I'm here to work with your boss. On a show that goes up TOMORROW. Are we good?"

Damien might have been a few years older than I was, but I was also a trained ATAC agent. I knew I could make him back down. He was angry now, I could see it on his face. He opened his mouth, but a yell from below stopped him.

"Damien!" Linden's voice echoed up the stairwell. "Where the heck are you?"

"Here Mr. von Louden!" Damien called back.

Heavy footsteps came racing up the steps. Linden was not happy.

"I've been looking for you for thirty minutes!" Linden's face was red and flushed from running up the steps. "I hope you have something better to do than sit around and chat all day."

"Yes, Mr. von Louden," stammered Damien.

"Take these," Linden said, yanking the glasses off his face. "They're broken. Again! I need them by tonight."

"Yes, sir."

"Now come with me. Do you have a pen on you? I need you to call Anthony at the catering place and make sure he has the order correct. Last time, they served shrimp. . . ."

Linden took off down the steps, and Damien had to run to keep up with him. I almost felt sorry for the kid. Almost. Then I remembered his questions, and the look in his eye, and I knew Damien thought we were up to something.

In truth, the feeling was mutual.

PRACTICE MAKES DEADLY

"Okay girls, one more time: step, kick, kick, step, down, and jump!"

Linden clicked a steady rhythm against the floor with his heel, and I tried my best to follow Claire as she floated gracefully across the rehearsal room. I kept my eyes on the mirror that took up one entire wall, making sure my lines were elegant and my face wasn't "twisted up like I tasted something sour," as Claire put it after the last run-through. I also did my best to ignore Bess and George giggling in the corner. I took a deep breath and followed Claire.

"Better!" Linden commented. "But you've got to hit that jump right on the beat."

Easy for you to say, I thought. *You're sitting down.*

Claire came over from the other side of the room. "Here, let me help you."

She stood behind me and put both hands on my hips. She nodded to Linden, who began his count again. This time, as we went through the moves, Claire kept her hands on me. A quarter of a second before Linden said "down," she pushed, and my knees bent. By the time he said "jump," I was already extending up through my toes, leaping into the air.

"Perfect!" said Linden. "You really are a natural at this. I'm very impressed."

Sweat dripped down my brow. It felt nice to hear, and in fact, I'd been pretty impressed with my skills myself. This wasn't the easiest stuff to learn, but I had a good memory and was generally physically skilled—I guess being a detective had some practical applications after all! But still, I was ready to do something other than these few steps over and over again. I looked around and made sure the door was closed.

"You guys remember this is just a cover story, right?" I asked.

"No understudy of mine is going to embarrass me onstage. At least, not again," said Claire. She paused for a moment, pulling from her bag one of her ever-present juice boxes—a new one that I'd purchased for her specially this morning. "Not that you'll be going on, but still. It's the principle."

She flopped heavily to the floor, and I joined her eagerly. I was so sore, I thought my blisters had blisters. Bess, George, and Linden joined us.

"Hey Nance," said Bess, "do you mind if George and I explore the theater? I mean, if that's okay with you, Mr. von Louden?"

Bess flashed her megawatt smile at Linden, and he returned one just as bright.

"Of course, girls," he replied. "Just try to stay out of the crew's way. Everyone is a little on edge. One day to go!"

That is putting it mildly, I thought. Everyone was walking around as though the stage were made of glass. No one wanted to be the next injury—especially now that there were real audiences coming to the show. Frank told me that last night's performance sold three times as many tickets as the night before Madonna was injured.

George and Bess promised to be careful. Their cover story as part of my "entourage" had so far guaranteed them access to most of the theater, and they were so personable, no one asked any questions. With a wave and a laugh, they exited the rehearsal room.

Since we were taking a break, Linden decided to get a few errands done around the theater. He told us to "take twenty" and disappeared out the door. Before it even closed behind him, I could hear him yelling for Damien. I was happy just to sit and massage my aching calves.

"Who's that?" I asked, as Claire stared at a small photo she'd taken from her bag. "Family?"

"An ancestor," said Claire. "But not family. Not blood family at least."

She smiled and turned the picture toward me. It was a black-and-white photo, clearly very old, of a woman in a glamorous gown.

"Who is she?" I asked.

"Alla Nazimova," replied Claire. "One of the early greats of the American stage. Once upon a time, she was the toast of Manhattan. Everyone knew her name. She's my inspiration. Her, Ethel Merman, Patty LuPone, Lea Salonga, Nell Carter—someday, my name is going to be on that list. The Great Women of the Stage."

I looked closely at the picture. The woman's eyes were dark and hooded. She looked mysterious, and somewhat sad. She was the opposite of Claire, who looked like a normal happy teen. Somewhere inside, however, I knew she had to be scared.

"Are you worried?" I asked.

Claire bit her lip and looked at the ground.

"I try not to let it get to me, you know? It's just . . . you never know what could happen."

I nodded sympathetically and scooted closer to where she sat. I put my arm around her.

"Frank and Joe are two of the best detectives I've ever met," I assured her. "And with me around to keep them on track, you've got nothing to worry about."

"What?" said Claire. "Oh, you mean the threats and stuff?" She stood up. "I'm not worried about that. That's part of life when you're a star. I thought you meant the show. It really isn't where I want it to be. Speaking of . . ."

She picked up her giant bag, which looked like the result of crossing a fancy gold purse with a duffel bag. She began pawing through it like a raccoon digging through trash.

"No, no, no, no . . ." Claire pulled out a curling iron, two books, a cookie wrapped in plastic, and a small troll doll. "How is this possible?" she muttered to herself. "Again!"

Claire looked through the bag more aggressively, pulling objects out left and right. Finally, with obvious frustration, she turned the bag upside down, pouring its contents on the floor.

"Where . . . is . . . it?!" she demanded angrily.

"What are you looking for?" I asked, gingerly pushing a pile of make-up around with my toe.

Claire jumped at the sound of my voice. Her furrowed brow smoothed out and she plastered a smile on her face.

"Oh, just my notebook," she said. "It has my entire track for the show blocked out: everywhere I have to stand, every move I have to perform, along with all my notes. I thought you might get some use out of it. I must have misplaced it though. Silly me."

Claire seemed the opposite of "silly" to me. And the way she was acting about this notebook made it clear that something was wrong. I took a shot in the dark.

"This . . . isn't the only thing that's gone missing recently, is it?"

Claire shrugged. I could tell someone had trained her to never be upset in public, but behind that mask of perfection, something was brewing. I waited, and sure enough, the truth burst out.

"No, it's not," she said finally. "I guess I've just been stressed out about this show. But I never lose things. Never! Why do you think I have such a huge bag? I'm basically a hoarder. If I didn't have a personal assistant, I'd end up on one of those reality shows where they come and clean your house and find possums living in the walls."

"Maybe someone is stealing from you?" I suggested off-handedly, wanting to see what she said.

"Maybe?" said Claire. "But it's all random stuff. Nothing worth money. You know what? Forget about it. We should get back to rehearsing anyway."

"Shouldn't we wait for Linden?" I didn't want to stop talking now that I'd finally started to get Claire to open up.

"It's cool," Claire smiled. She swooped down and touched her toes, then slowly rolled back up until she was standing straight. "We're going to work on stage combat. First things first—do you know how to take a fall?"

Finally! I thought. *Something I know.*

"Try me," I said, smiling back at Claire.

The next hour passed quickly. Linden checked on us once, then told us to continue—he'd be back soon. Combat was something I was all too familiar with, and Claire turned out to be a great sparring partner. Stage fighting is sort of the opposite of a real fight, since your goal is never to hit the other person—or at least not to hit them hard. But it was pretty similar to the real thing.

Claire and I fought back and forth across the rehearsal room. She put me in a headlock and I slapped her face. I swept a leg out from under her and she punched me in the stomach. It was the most fun I'd had all day.

So when someone yanked my shoulder from behind, my natural instincts took over.

"Hee-ya!" I yelled, as I grabbed the person's wrist and pulled forward, tossing them over my hip and slamming them straight into the floor.

BAM!

CHAPTER 9

FRANK

A SUSPECT RECOVERS

After Bess and George let me out of the basement, I decided to join them on part of their tour—mostly because I wanted an excuse to see the entire crew. If anyone looked at me funny, it could be a clue about who locked me down in the basement. Jason told me the door was known for shutting accidentally, but I doubted it was also known for leaving threatening notes.

We headed upstairs to the backstage area, but we hadn't gone far before a scream ripped through the theater.

"Nancy!" Bess, George, and I said simultaneously. Nancy's scream hit high notes that even the biggest Broadway diva would be jealous of. There was no mistaking it for anyone else.

"Come on!" yelled George, racing past a miniature Eiffel Tower and three backup dancers dressed as nurses. "This way."

We raced through the rehearsal room door just in time to see Claire and Nancy help Linden to his feet. Joe was just behind us.

"Is everything okay?" I asked.

"Yes!" snapped Linden.

"Oh man, I'm so sorry!" said Nancy. "When you came up behind me, I just—"

"Just what?" he shouted. "Decided to break my skull?"

"No!" said Nancy. "You surprised me, that's all."

Linden took a deep breath and exhaled slowly. He yanked his glasses off, cleaned them angrily on his shirt, and then shoved them back on his face. He tried his best to smile, but it didn't work.

"I was just trying to help with your stage combat," he said, rubbing the back of his head. "But it looks like you're all set in that area."

"HA!" Laughter erupted out of Claire like lava from a volcano. "She TOSSED you. I mean, you went flying."

"I'm aware of that Claire," said Linden. He gave her a sharp look that she didn't even notice.

"No, but like—she threw you across the room. You've got to be, what, six inches taller than she is? That was hysterical."

I could see Linden's hands balling into fists at his side.

Everything I'd read online about Linden von Louden had said that the biggest threat to his career was his temper, and it looked like we were about to get a front row seat to that show.

But somehow, he stopped himself. He uncurled his fists finger by finger. He took a deep breath.

"Thankfully, I'm fine," he said. "No harm no foul, right? Let's get back to rehearsal."

"The understudy slams the director." Laurel's voice floated into the room from behind me. I turned to find her leaning against the door frame with her phone in hand. "Great, just what this show needs. New injuries."

Linden turned on her, his face filled with fury.

"You shut up!" he snarled.

"Fine," said Laurel. "I don't have time to talk, anyway. Some of us have work to do."

"What did you say?" said Linden, his voice dangerously quiet. He yanked his glasses off and cleaned them again. It seemed like all the anger he'd been bottling up from Claire and Nancy had found a new target.

"You heard me," said Laurel.

"How dare you!?" Linden screamed. His face was red and angry. He rubbed his glasses harder, and this time they broke at the bridge.

"Broke your glasses again, eh?" mocked Laurel. "You should just buy stock in Gorilla Glue." With that, she sauntered out of the room.

"Darn it!" Linden yelled. "Where is Damien? Why is no one working? And where is the Gorilla Glue?!"

He stormed after Laurel. As he passed through the door, he turned back for a second.

"Just . . . rehearse something!"

The room was tense and silent after they left. We all met each other's eyes and nodded, except for Claire, who had pulled a granola bar from her bag and was busy tearing the wrapper off with her teeth.

"There's something off about those two," I said, echoing what everyone was thinking.

"Word," said Claire. "The negative vibes off the two of them! It's like every night they're auditioning for the Scottish play."

I stared at Claire blankly. "*The* Scottish play? Isn't there more than one Scottish play?"

"You know," she said with a mouth full of granola. "THE Scottish play. The famous one. By Shakespeare?"

"Oh, you mean *Macbeth*?" said Nancy.

"Noooo!" howled Claire. She dropped her granola bar to the ground. Joe leapt forward.

"Are you okay? Was there something in that bar? Frank, call an ambulance!"

"No!" yelled Claire. Her eyes were wild and her hands were shaking. She backed away from all of us. "It's her! She said it."

Claire pointed at Nancy.

"All she said was Mac—"

"STOP!" shouted Claire. "Never say that name in the theater. It's the worst luck imaginable."

Considering that she'd already been poisoned, and that her understudy had broken both her legs, I didn't know how much worse luck this show could have.

"Don't tell me you believe in those sorts of superstitions?" said Joe with a laugh.

Claire turned on him. "This is not just superstition. My friend Tia was in a show where the technical director talked about *that* play right before opening night, and one of the drops caught fire in the second act!"

Nancy held up her hands as if she was dealing with a wild animal. Slowly, she stepped toward Claire. "There has to be something we can do."

Claire nodded. "You have to go outside and run around the theater three times. Counterclockwise. And then spit."

"Okay," said Nancy.

Claire made a little motion with her hand, shooing Nancy off.

"Right now?" asked Nancy.

With a nod from Claire, Nancy sighed and headed outside.

"That was awesome," said George, laughing. "Does everyone in the theater call it the Scottish play?"

"Oh, yes," said Claire, who was calmer now. "We're

very serious about all of this. The theater is an ancient tradition, you know. And as artists, we've always been a little closer to ghosts and gods and things not of this world."

Claire waxed poetic about the theater and George lost interest quickly. She rolled her eyes and winked at me. George thought superstitions were interesting. But pretentions? Not so much.

Heavy footsteps announced Nancy's return. Claire ran across the room and stopped her in the doorway.

"You ran all the way around three times?"

"Yes, Claire."

"Counterclockwise?"

"Yes, Claire."

"And you remembered to spit?"

"Yes!"

"Okay, then you can come back in."

Claire stepped out of the way and let Nancy in. As she did, her cell phone began to ring. I couldn't help but notice that her ring tone was the theme music from her TV show—which was also the single off her first album.

"Oh no," said Claire, looking at the screen. "It's *her*! Ugh. Let me get rid of her—this will just take a minute."

She closed her eyes for a second, and all traces of irritation vanished. When she answered the phone, her voice was bright and perky. This was the weirdest part of working with actors—how well they lied.

"Hi!" said Claire with excitement. "I was just thinking about calling you. The flowers? Oh good, I'm glad you liked them."

She turned toward us, pulled the phone away from her mouth, and pretended to hang herself. But the whole time, her voice was chipper and friendly.

"Great! Great. Your role? Well, you'd have to talk to Linden about that. Speaking of, I have to get back to rehearsal. No. No. No, you're the best! Love ya like a sister."

She clicked the phone closed, though even from across the room I could tell the other person on the line was still talking.

"Who was that?" I asked. Whoever it was, Claire clearly didn't like them. And it seemed like they had no idea. Claire insisted she didn't have any enemies, but I wondered if she was just too self-centered to notice.

"Madonna," Claire said. "Not the famous one. Apparently she's like conscious again? And she wants her part back. Can you believe that? She was never very good, and now she has two broken legs. Although, come to think of it, that could only improve her dancing."

"I guess you're not the president of her fan club, eh?" said Nancy.

"Funny you should say that," Claire replied, throwing her arm around Nancy's shoulder. Now that Madonna was back in the picture, Nancy's *Macbeth* slipup seemed to be forgotten.

"Madonna actually used to be the president of *my* fan club, until she got the role as my understudy. I wish they'd never cast her. It's like they hired me a second shadow!"

She threw her hands in the air in frustration.

"If she's awake, we should go talk to her," Joe said to me. "You girls will be safe here?"

"With this one around, we've got nothing to worry about," said Claire, punching Nancy in the arm. "You should have seen her stage combat! Besides, we have to get back to rehearsing anyway."

"You guys go," said Nancy. "But we should meet up later and talk."

I nodded. From the sound of her voice, Nancy had some information for us.

"If it's all right with you, Nance, we're going to continue our tour." Bess said.

"Sure," said Nancy. "But you know what, you should have someone with you, just in case. Do you think Linden would mind if Damien showed them around?" Nancy asked Claire.

"Nah," Claire responded. "That little weirdo's got nothing better to do."

Very clever, I thought. That made one suspect who wasn't going to have the time to cause any new mischief.

"And you two will stay here rehearsing?" I asked. Thinking about Madonna's accident had me worried for Nancy's safety.

"Of course—"

"AAAHHHHHHH!!!!" Claire screamed suddenly. "NO!"

CHAPTER *10*

J O E

ACT ONE: CONFESSION!

Everyone froze. Claire's scream echoed in the room. She had one heck of a powerful voice for such a small person! I ran to her side so fast it was as if I teleported.

"What's wrong?" I asked. I was always ready to play fair prince to a damsel in distress, especially one as cute as Claire. Nancy and Frank were right behind me.

"Look at this!" she howled, thrusting her phone at me.

The screen showed a text message from an unknown number.

"DROP OUT—OR DROP DEAD!!!!!"

"It's okay," said Frank, trying to sound reassuring. "We're going to catch this creep."

"Okay?" yelled Claire, only a little less loudly than

she'd screamed before. "This is the opposite of okay! What part of this seems okay to you?"

She stomped over to the corner where all her stuff appeared to be piled on the ground. All the while she stared at the screen.

"If they think they can scare me off like this, they have another think coming," she muttered to herself. "I'm calling my agent. No, I'm issuing a press release!"

She dialed her phone rapidly as she stuffed her things back into her purse. "Get me Stanley. No I won't hold. This is Claire Cleveland. CLEVELAND."

She put her hand over the mouthpiece. "Assistants," she said. "He runs through them like tissues. I'm going to my dressing room."

Nancy started to say something, but Claire interrupted her.

"Relax, I had my first stalker in kindergarten," she said. "Don't worry, I'll lock the door."

Yelling at her agent, she trooped out.

"She's intense!" I said. I liked her spunk.

"You should try fighting with her," Nancy said, rubbing her shoulder. "She's got a good right hook, too."

"Find anything out?" Frank asked.

"Not much," Nancy shrugged. "But I think someone is stealing her stuff. She said a couple of things have gone missing from her purse recently, including her journal with all of her notes on the show. You guys got anything?"

"There was some sticky stuff on the plane," Frank said. "And someone locked me down there and left this helpful note for me."

He pulled out a piece of paper with the word "LEAVE" scrawled on it in black marker.

"Claire was definitely poisoned—Vijay confirmed her juice boxes were tampered with. Want to know the last person who definitely touched them?"

We all nodded.

"Damien." I mimed dribbling a ball, then slam-dunked it in the air. "And the crowd goes wild! Joe Hardy with another fantastic play."

"Great," sighed Bess. "Have you set us up as babysitters for yet another crazy?"

"Don't think of yourselves as babysitters," said Nancy. "Think of yourselves as . . ."

"Prison guards?" prompted George.

"That doesn't sound much better," said Bess. "Do guards get tips?"

"Go," said Nancy, laughing. "I'm going to stick around here. I'm sure when Claire gets off the phone, she and Linden will want to get back to rehearsal."

We said our good-byes and headed out.

The next morning, we went out to visit Madonna bright and early.

"I love this city!" I said, as we passed three men

dressed like superheroes. They were carrying briefcases, and aside from the spandex, looked as if they were headed to work. Next to them, a wedding party was being pulled down Broadway in a series of horse-drawn carriages. "I mean, don't get me wrong, Bayport is awesome. But New York City is . . . New York City!"

"Huh?" said Frank, who was too busy staring at his phone to appreciate any of the awesomeness that was all around us. "Right. What you said."

I recognized the tone in his voice instantly. It was Frank's I'm-thinking-about-something-on-a-case-and-not-really-paying-attention-to-you-Joe voice. I heard it a lot.

"What is it?" I asked.

Frank handed me his phone as we dodged through the crowds in Times Square.

"Look at this photo," he said. "Look familiar?"

"Whoa! That dude's getting wasted by a chick."

I looked more closely.

"Oh, snap! That's Nancy and Linden. You took that?" I asked.

Frank shook his head.

"Vijay forwarded it to me. Apparently, it showed up on a website called Broadway Buzz last night. It was headlined UNKNOWN ACTRESS SLAMS DIRECTOR. It's already been picked up by two major news agencies."

My heart sank. This wasn't good news.

"At least you can't really make out her face," I said, staring at the photo. As detectives, it was never a good idea to get in the papers *before* the case was done. You never knew who might get tipped off, or recognize you later. "Who do you think took it? And who put it up?"

Frank grimaced.

"That's the worst part. This isn't the only photo out there. Look!"

Frank scrolled down, showing me images of the fiery plane, an injured Madonna being carried out of the theater, and a host of other accidents that had happened on the set of *Wake*.

"Who's always around the set, with her phone at the ready?" I murmured, half to myself.

"Laurel," said Frank, and I nodded agreement. "That's what I'm thinking too. No one else was in that rehearsal room, unless Bess is a secret celebrity blogger."

"But why would Laurel do that? Is she out to sink the show?"

"I don't know. Why would she bring us in to protect Claire if she's the one harassing her?" Frank wondered.

"What if Linden forced her to bring us on board?" I answered.

"What if Linden is in on it? They are brother and sister, after all . . ."

Frank trailed off, lost in thought, staring at all the gossip photos. Finally, he clicked his phone shut.

"Man!" he said. "The list of suspects on this one is just getting longer and longer. Maybe Madonna can shed some light on all this."

We'd arrived at her hospital, an impressive complex of glass and pink stone buildings that took up more than an entire city block. Over the automatic doors, the sign read BELLEVUE. A cluster of doctors and nurses were chatting across the street, as a steady stream of patients and families—some anxious, some excited, some tired—moved briskly through the entrance.

We walked up to the front desk, where a woman in green scrubs sat behind a computer. Her nametag read DOLORES. For five minutes, she acted as though we weren't there.

"Excuse me?" I said finally. "We're here to see . . ."

"Visiting hours don't start for another fifteen minutes," she interrupted me without looking away from the screen. Was everyone in New York like this? "Name?"

"I'm Joe Hardy, and this is my brother Frank."

Her eyes flicked away from the computer screen for a second, giving me a look of contempt. "Not your name. The patient's name."

"Madonna de la Varga," I replied. If Dolores wanted to keep this short and sweet, I could play that game too.

Dolores tapped on her keyboard for a few minutes. The ancient yellowed printer on the desk next to her slowly rattled to life.

"These are your visitor passes," she said, pulling two poorly printed labels out of the printer. "Show them to the guard on the seventh floor."

And with that, Dolores forgot we existed.

We grabbed some candy bars from the vending machines, because sleuthing is definitely hungry work. Then we took the elevator up. Security on the seventh floor didn't seem to care that we were ten minutes early for visiting hours.

HA! I thought, as we walked down the long, masking-tape-colored hallway. *Take that, Dolores.*

Madonna was sitting up in bed when we arrived. Both her legs were in solid white casts, but her makeup and hair looked professionally done, and the room was ringed with flowers.

"Welcome!" she said as we walked in, as though she were the host of some game show. "Now, don't tell me your names. I always remember my fans. Joe and . . . Frank, was it?"

We nodded.

"You're working with Linden and Laurel, right? That's lovely. Did you come here for an autograph, or did they send you to tell me when I could come back to the show? I've been thinking that the part could really work well with me in a wheelchair. I sent them a few e-mails about the idea, but I haven't heard back from them yet. Do you know what they're thinking? They haven't gotten another understudy yet, have they?"

Madonna talked so fast that there was hardly a chance to get a word in edgewise. But she had to breathe at some point.

"Actually, we are working with Linden and Laurel," Frank began.

"But not in the way you think," I continued. "We work for an organization called American Teens Against Crime. The von Loudens asked us to pose as high school students in order to find out who has been threatening Claire."

Madonna's face turned white. *Poor girl!* I thought. Bad enough to be injured at work and lose her job, but now it turned out it was a murder attempt!

"We need to ask you a few questions Madonna," Frank said.

Tears welled up in her eyes. Before we could say another word, Madonna burst out.

"Okay!" she said, her voice breaking with fear. "You've caught me. I did it. Please, please don't send me to jail!"

Then she started sobbing.

CHAPTER 11

NANCY

LOOKING UP

"Let me go!" I yelled, struggling against the man who held me from behind. He had his arms around me in a bear hug. I threw myself to the left, and he staggered, suddenly off balance. His grip weakened, and I slipped free.

"Now," I said, pointing a gun at his head. "You will tell me everything you know."

"STOP!" yelled Claire, who was sitting in the director's chair while Linden played the part opposite me. "The line is 'you had better tell me everything you know, you traitor!' We have to let the audience know that he isn't just some run-of-the-mill Nazi. He's a turn-coat. An informer. The lowest of the low!"

Claire was so in character she was nearly foaming

at the mouth! I wasn't sure whether to admire her or worry for Linden's safety.

"You have good intonation, though," said Linden with a smile. He stretched his arms. "And you're strong for your size," he said, impressed.

I shook my head with frustration. "You traitor, you traitor, you traitor," I mumbled to myself. I'd gotten it right in the last take—but I'd forgotten to draw my gun. I've never really liked weapons, especially firearms. The take before that I'd done everything perfectly, but I hadn't remembered to face out toward the audience while doing it. Acting was much, much harder than it looked. Still, being a detective had taught me to have a good memory, or else I would have been totally lost.

Linden, Claire, and I had been working on the same scene since Linden had returned from his fight with Laurel yesterday. Whatever had happened between them, Linden was in a better mood afterward—or at least a more focused one. Apparently, Claire was weakest on the first act of the play, so he'd decided to concentrate on that. That way, we could both be learning at the same time. So that was what we had done for the rest of yesterday, and we'd jumped right back into the first act this morning—which was good, since the official opening night was this evening, and it sounded like the show was going to sell out! I was just glad there was no way I was going on.

"Claire, you want to give the scene a try?" Linden asked. The tone in his voice made it clear that it wasn't really a request.

"No," said Claire. She'd settled back into his chair. "I'm kind of enjoying being the director for a change."

I could hear Linden's frustration in the way he blew his breath out through his nose loudly. He yanked his newly repaired glasses off his face.

"Are . . . you . . . sure?" he tried again, each word crisp and angry.

Claire nodded. She was testing him, I could tell—you don't make it far as a private detective if you don't know how to read people. All the signs I got from Linden showed he was headed toward a massive explosion. His face was red, his knuckles were white, and his eyes were tight and small. According to Frank, he had a pretty well-known temper, and a lot of the research I did online before getting here said that he blew up at his actors all the time.

Which is why I was surprised when he suddenly unclenched his hands, clapped Claire on the shoulder, and laughed.

"Very funny," he said. "Now come on. We need you on that stage tonight, ready to wow the audience. This is the show's biggest night."

Claire smiled up at him. "Well, when you put it that way . . . all right," she said.

If Linden still looked like he was carrying about a

million pounds of tension between his shoulder blades, at least he hadn't taken it out on Claire. Or me!

Linden had us run the scene again, this time with me playing the Nazi. Then we ran it again. Then again. And again. And againagainagainagainagainagainagain!

By the time Bess and George returned, I was on the verge of going crazy. How many times could they do the same ten minutes' worth of dialog?

"How are you doing?" I asked, eager to hear someone say something other than "you traitor" or "cut!"

"Great!" said Bess, bouncing over to me. "Sorry, Mr. Linden—are we interrupting?"

But Linden just smiled. "We needed a break anyway," he said. "Claire, Nancy, take five."

Either the Internet was full of lies, or someone had taken an anger management class. Or both.

"Actually, we were wondering if we could take Nancy away for an hour or so?" said George, who was half hiding behind Bess. "We wanted to show her some of the other parts of the theater. You know . . . before opening night."

I could tell from the way she said it that they had something specific in mind to show me. Their plan had been to go over the theater inch by inch, since Damien had given them a good idea of the layout on his tour yesterday. I wondered what they had found, and how Frank and Joe's talk with Madonna was going.

"Ahhhh," said Linden. "You're—how do they say it in the movies? 'Casing the joint.'"

George winced, but continued smiling. "Yup! Is that cool?"

"Certainly," said Linden. "Claire and I could use some time to ourselves, anyway. You girls go."

"You two will stay right here in this room, right?" As much as I wanted to get out of there and see whatever it was that Bess and George had found, I had to make sure Claire wasn't going to run off alone. Claire nodded absentmindedly, focusing on the notes Linden had given from their last run through.

"Don't worry, Nancy," Linden said quietly. "I'll have my eye on her the whole time."

George and Bess practically pulled me out the door. After the quiet of the padded rehearsal room, the energy backstage on opening night was almost overwhelming. Everywhere I looked dancers were practicing, racks of costumes were flying, last-minute adjustments were being made, and people were running back and forth carrying props and binders. It was amazing to see how much tightly controlled chaos it took to make a Broadway show happen.

"So what's up?" I asked. "Did you find something?"

"Not exactly," said Bess. "I spent most of my time checking out the sound system. Did you know there's a microphone that when you speak into it, everyone with one of those," Bess pointed to the tiny ear sets most of the crew were wearing, "will hear you all at once? They call it the 'God mic.'"

That was cool, but not really worth pulling me away from Claire.

"Ignore her," said George. "She just wants to get one of those for herself. Plus, she actually spent most of her time checking out Tim, the scenic designer who was showing her the mics."

Bess blushed, but didn't disagree.

"I, on the other hand, found something you actually need to see," George continued.

"What is it?" I asked, excited.

George pointed up above our heads. I craned my neck.

"All I see is a mess of wires and pipes and things." I said, hesitantly. I wasn't sure what I was looking at.

"We were talking to Tim, Bess's new friend," said George, pointing to a cute, curly-haired guy who was operating a saw over in one corner. "He told me there's a whole world up there in 'the grid.' It's designed to make it possible for the people running the lights and things to get around during the show—without being seen by the audience."

A lightbulb went off in my head.

"So if I wanted to mess with Claire during the show . . ."

"You'd hide up there!" Bess and George said at the same time. "That's why we came and got you," George continued. "Come on."

George and Bess brought me to the tiny metal staircase that led up into the rigging. The higher we went, the quieter the noises of the theater became, until it was just a distant roar below us. It was dark and quiet and downright creepy up here. Lights and props and planes loomed in the dark, balanced carefully on thin metal wires.

"Wow," I said, walking down the narrow walkway that led from the stairs out into the grid proper. "This is intense!"

"Right?" said George. "As soon as Tim told me about it, my danger-senses started tingling."

"Tiiiiim this, Tiiiiim that," said Bess. "I think you're the one with a crush!"

George's mouth dropped open. "I don't . . . it's not . . . he's just . . . I'm going to look over there!" she sputtered, heading quickly down a walkway that intersected the one we were on.

"George and Tim sitting in a tree, k-i-s-s-i-n-g . . ." sang Bess to herself as we walked. I smiled. Bess and George were both best friends and cousins—they really knew how to push each other's buttons. Rarely did they like the same boys, though, and if I knew my friends, Bess was going to take advantage of this moment to tease George mercilessly.

I peered beneath my feet. The walkway was made out of thin strips of steel laid out in a diamond pattern, so I could see all the way to the seats below. It was a long way down, and I shivered just thinking about the drop. Someone was walking beneath me, and I could imagine the terrible injuries they would receive if something fell on them from this height.

Wait a second! I realized. *That's Linden!*

Even from up here, I could recognize his perfect blond hair and easy, in-charge walk. He'd promised me he'd stay with Claire. What was he doing in the front of the house? Then I noticed the long trail of people carrying cameras behind him. He must have been leading a press tour. I couldn't blame him for that . . . but it definitely made me antsy, knowing Claire was alone.

Bess and I reached the end of the first walkway. We were now standing dead center over the stage. The practicing backup dancers looked like tiny windup toy soldiers. Another narrow path stretched out perpendicular to our own. Without a word, we split up. I went right, Bess went left. That was one of the best parts about working with my two best friends: We were often so in sync we didn't even need to talk things over.

I'd only gone about fifteen feet when something strange caught my eye. The walkways had handrails running on either side of them, held up by narrow metal poles. At the base of one of the poles, someone had left a pile of . . . stuff. I knelt down to look more closely. There was a candle, a lock of hair, a pink plaid scrunchie, and one of Claire's headshots! The headshot was taped to the pole, and everything else was arranged before it. It looked like an altar—a weird, deranged altar!

I looked down at the stage below. I couldn't be certain, but I was willing to bet we were right above the mark where Claire was supposed to start the play. Whatever creepy stalker had built this altar had found the best spot from which to spy on Claire—or kill her. We had to find out who had put this stuff here, and get ahold of them before the show started in a few hours!

Just as I stood up, a shout came from the other end of the grid. I whirled around to see George bent over the railing. She was holding on to a rope with both hands. Something heavy must have been on the other end, because her entire body was straining with the effort of keeping it up.

"Nancy!" George yelled. "Help!"

George stumbled, and the rope pulled her a little farther over the edge. Now she was standing on tiptoe. In a few seconds, she would either have to let go—or get pulled over the edge!

"I'm coming!" I yelled, racing down the narrow walkway at top speed. In the dark, my foot caught one of the poles, and I slammed my knee hard into the metal. It was all I could do not to stop and grab my leg, but I gritted my teeth and just kept running.

Inch by inch, George was being pulled over the railing. Whatever she was holding must have been incredibly heavy.

"Hang on, George!" yelled Bess, who was running over from the other direction. We both made it to George at the same time and grabbed the rope from either side. Heaving with all we had, we gave George enough support to get her feet fully back on the ground. Whatever was at the end of that rope must have weighed a ton. Even with the three of us pulling as hard as we could, we couldn't raise it back up. After a minute of wrestling with it, my arm muscles were beginning to burn. We couldn't do this for much longer. And when we let go, whatever we were holding would slam into the busy stage below. I looked down and saw a dozen actors scurrying across the stage like ants, oblivious to the danger they were in. I wasn't going to let anything happen to them.

"Bess, George—if I let go for a second, can the two of you hold it up?" I asked.

George nodded.

"Make it a really, really quick second," Bess grunted. "This is definitely not part of my usual gym routine."

"Ready?" I asked. "One, two, . . . three!"

Bess and George leaned back, trying to use their own weight to make up for the fact that I was no longer holding the rope with them. I could tell they wouldn't be able to keep it up for long.

I grabbed the slack coil of rope that was still on the walkway. Quickly, I wrapped it around one of the poles three times, finishing it off with a tight knot. It might not hold forever, but it would work for now.

"That was too close!" I said, as George and Bess let go and began massaging their sore arms. "What's on the other end of this thing?"

George sat down heavily, sweat pouring down her face. "It's one of . . . the bomber doors," she panted. "Real World War II ones . . . Linden insisted."

"What happened?" I asked, bending down to peer more closely at the rope. I hardly needed George to answer. It was easy to see where it had been cut nearly in two. Whoever had done this had set it like a booby trap. At some point, the rest of the rope would have torn, and whoever happened to be below it would have been crushed to death! George had come along just in time.

"I was looking at this when I noticed the rope fraying," George said, holding up a brown notebook with a bookmark inside it. "I think it's Claire's."

I flipped it open to the bookmarked page. It was Claire's all right. In fact, it was her missing show journal, the one she'd offered to lend me. The marked page contained her notes on her entrance in the second act, when she was supposed to "parachute" onstage through these very bomber doors. I had been wrong before. This wasn't a random trap. It was built so that Claire's additional weight would break the rope, sending her—and the doors—tumbling sixty feet to the stage below! We had to get downstairs and warn somebody before my knot gave.

I heard the clink of metal on metal behind us, and I whirled around. While we had been fighting with the rope, Damien had crept up behind us. Now he stood between us and the ladder back down.

"What are you doing up here?" he said, his voice low and menacing.

That's when I noticed that in his right hand he held a vicious, sharp-looking saw.

ACT TWO: THE REAL TRUTH

I stared at Madonna in shock, my mouth hanging open. She was the one trying to kill Claire? Here we thought she was an innocent bystander! We'd spent the past few days investigating everyone at the theater, and our saboteur was already far away. And from the look of her casts, while Madonna might not have been imprisoned, she wasn't going anywhere anytime soon.

"You did it?" Joe asked.

"Yes!" moaned Madonna. Her voice had gotten hoarse and low. "It was me. Me! Oh what will my parents think? And my fans? And Claire!"

She thrust her wrists out toward us.

"Cuff me! Take me away. I belong in jail for this."

I leaned forward to take her hand and comfort her,

and she pulled them back as fast as she could. "No!" she screamed. "I'm too delicate! I'll never survive a jail sentence! My life is . . . ruined!"

With that, she collapsed backward onto the bed, tears streaming down her face. I couldn't help but notice that she took a moment to arrange her hair so that it perfectly framed her face on the pillow. There was something odd going on here. I was beginning to feel as if I was in some sort of terrible soap opera—the teary confessions, the hospital setting, the terrible acting . . .

"So, you—" I started to ask Madonna a question, but she popped back up before I got two words out.

"I just couldn't resist," she said quietly. She made her eyes big and innocent looking, and she peered up at us as though she were a child being punished by her parents. She seemed to be in a different movie now, no longer a soap opera. "I wanted to feel the lights and the applause. You understand that, don't you?"

She grabbed my hand in both of hers. A single tear slipped down her cheek.

"I'm so sorry," she said. "I know it was wrong to put that stuff in Claire's juice. But she was never going to be sick. This is my first role on Broadway and I was never going to get onstage! I thought, if I did it during the preview, it wouldn't be so bad. And the guy at the pharmacy said that ipecac was medicine, and a little bit would never really hurt anyone. She is okay, right? Oh no—is that why you're here? Did she die? I'll never forgive myself if I killed Claire Cleveland. Why is this happening to me?"

Madonna's words became garbled into one long sobbing sound, which broke off suddenly.

"Do they need me to take over the part?" she asked eagerly. "Because I've been thinking, we could put Nancy Wake in a wheelchair, and the play would totally still work. I've mapped out all the choreography in my head. It'll just need minor changes. I can be at the theater in thirty minutes. Twenty, if you two will give me a hand."

Madonna started fumbling with her hospital bed, trying to free her broken legs from the restraints that held them in place.

I couldn't believe what I was hearing. Madonna was crazy. She'd spent the last few weeks trying to threaten and kill Claire, and now she thought they'd let her back onstage?

"I'm sorry, Madonna, but that's not possible," I said. She tried to interrupt me, but I talked right over her. "You're going to be arrested for harassment, theft, and attempted murder."

It was harsh, but there seemed to be no other way to get through to her. Now it was Madonna's turn to stare at us in shock.

"But . . . but . . . but . . . I never stole anything from anyone! Or threatened anyone. All I did was put ipecac in her drink, once, I swear!"

Joe and I exchanged a look. This was getting interesting.

"So you had nothing to do with the plane being set on fire?" Joe asked. "Or the threatening texts Claire has been receiving?"

Madonna flinched, and this time, it seemed genuine. "Heck no!" she said, with a sudden thick New York accent that she had been hiding this whole time. "Claire's my idol! I've wanted to be her since I first saw her on the Ratty-Rat Club on TV when I was a kid. This is my dream job! I would never hurt her."

I quirked my eyebrow at her.

"Well, I would never hurt her in a *real* way," Madonna clarified. "I dream about being her some day. Claire Cleveland," Madonna sighed, "is the luckiest girl in America."

Wow. She was definitely a Claire fan. There was no faking that kind of emotion. What was with this play? I guess Claire had more star power than I realized. Between the rabid fans outside, and the even more rabid fans in the cast and crew, she must have had the most dedicated fan club in the world.

I pulled over a chair from the other side of the room and took a seat. This was starting to make my head swim. Joe perched at the end of Madonna's hospital bed.

"You swear that's all you did?" asked Joe. Madonna nodded. For the first time, I felt as if we were seeing her real personality—the star-struck girl from Brooklyn who made it big by accident. She wasn't our killer. But she might have some useful information.

"Did you see anything strange before you fell through the trap?" I asked. "Was anything off, or anyone acting weird?"

"Nuh-uh," said Madonna. "I was flawless, and the show was going great. It was the best night of my life. Well, maybe that was the day I got cast. Or that time a girl mistook me for J.Lo . . ."

"Nothing strange happened during the preview?" I asked again, trying to keep her on topic.

Madonna thought hard for a moment. She was one of those people who couldn't think something, or feel something, without it showing up on her face, so Joe and I watched while she tried to remember.

"No," she said finally. "I mean, let's face it, the show is kind of a mess at the moment. The dancers were a little off. They kept messing up the routine, which threw me off a little. They were just a nightmare, especially that blond one. But they only threw me off a little!" she quickly clarified. "Please don't send me to jail," she said miserably. "This isn't my fault!"

She sounded defensive, and I got the sense that in her world *nothing* was ever Madonna's fault. But she might also have been right. I looked at Joe. Madonna had done wrong, but her punishment was ten times worse than any harm she'd intended. Joe nodded slightly.

"Look," I said, trying to sound firm but understanding. "You know what you did was wrong, right?"

Madonna nodded.

"You can't come back to the show. But this"—I waved at her broken legs—"seems like punishment enough for what you did. Do you agree?"

Joe nodded.

"So are we good?" I asked, trying to sound as stern as possible.

"Yes, I—"

"Good." I cut Madonna off. We didn't have time for another speech. If she wasn't our killer, someone else was, and we needed to get back to the theater and find out who. "We're leaving—I don't want to see you again. Is that clear?"

"Yes," Madonna said. "Sir," she added after a second's pause.

As we walked out of the hospital room, I looked back and saw her frantically typing away on her cell phone. Something told me her version of our little visit was going to be all over the web within minutes—if it wasn't already. Madonna seemed to be quite the fast typist.

"Do you think she's telling the truth?" I asked Joe as we left the hospital.

He thought for a second. "Yeah," he said. "She might be a drama queen, but I think she was honest with us at the end."

That was my read on it too. Joe and I might have our differences, but when it came to our cases, we were like-minded.

"What is with all of these people and their obsession with Claire?" I wondered out loud. Maybe it was just that in our work with ATAC we met a lot of famous people, but celebrity obsessions didn't make much sense to me. They were just people, after all. Busy, rich, sometimes talented people—but people nonetheless. Some were nice and some were mean, but none of them deserved to be worshipped the way so many people seemed to worship Claire.

On the street, my pocket started buzzing. My heart jumped. What if it was Nancy, calling us because something was happening at the theater? Today was opening night, after all, and if our killer was going to make a move, it had to happen soon. Luckily, it was just Vijay.

"Hey hey hey," he said as I picked up. "You were right."

"Always," I said. "What was I right about this time?"

"It's Vijay," I mouthed to Joe. He gave me the thumbs up, and we continued walking as Vijay and I talked.

"That sticky stuff you found in the airplane engine compartment? It's definitely a fire accelerant. It's kind of clever, really. All they had to do was smear the inside of the compartment with that stuff. Once the engine got going, it was just a matter of time until the heat made the chemicals combust. Then, *poof!* It's World War II all over again."

I'd almost forgotten that we'd sent the sample off to ATAC to be analyzed. Madonna might have been a bust, but maybe this would be the clue to crack the case.

"Any idea what chemical our would-be arsonist was using?"

"Yup, it's . . . uhhh . . . hold on one second. I wrote it down somewhere. It had a funny name. I'll find it."

I could hear the sound of mounds of paper being rifled through, and the occasional electronic beeping noise that seemed to follow Vijay wherever he was. He had so many computers on him at all times that he was one small step away from being a cyborg.

"Ape Affixer?" he mumbled. "Monkey Mud? It was something like that. I'm going to find it, I swear."

But I didn't think he needed to. I was pretty sure I knew what it was.

"Gorilla Glue?" I said.

"Yes!" he shouted. "Ding ding ding! What is that stuff

anyway? I thought you were working on Broadway, not at the Bronx Zoo."

"You'd be surprised how similar the two are. . . ." I told him. "Anyway, Gorilla Glue is an adhesive, a kind of really strong glue they use a lot backstage. And I think I know someone who has it. Good work Veej."

"Always," replied Vijay. He was nothing if not humble. "Anything else I can do you for?"

"Yes, actually—can you run a trace for me on a text message?"

"Joe gave me the number already. Death threats for your prima ballerina, right? It's a prepaid cell phone, bought in cash near the theater. Dead end. If you can let me know when it's in use, or might still be on, I can track it. But when it's off, there's no way."

Rats. I'd been doing pretty well there for a second. Still, one clue was better than a grand total of none.

I said good-bye to Vijay and turned to Joe.

"Vijay says it was Gorilla Glue inside the engine."

"That sounds really familiar. Where have I heard of that before?"

"It's the stuff that's holding together Linden's glasses. Remember who's in charge of fixing them?"

"Damien!" Joe yelled. "It's been that little weirdo all along! We need to warn the girls, and get back to the theater pronto. Opening night curtain call is in a few hours!"

"Let's not leap to any conclusions," I cautioned Joe, although I was pretty sure he was right. "After all, we still have some big questions for Laurel, too."

"Either way, we need to get back to that theater!" replied Joe. He was running before he'd even finished the sentence.

CHAPTER **13**

JOE

OPENING NIGHT JITTERS

We ran back so fast that I was almost winded by the time we arrived. Almost. I am Joe Hardy, after all.

The crowd outside the theater was out of control—a mass of crazy fans, paparazzi, and ambulance chasers who wanted to be able to say they were there the night someone tried to kill Claire Cleveland. It didn't help that the show had a ticket lottery: Each night ten randomly chosen fans would get free seats. There were tons of people camping out just for the chance to see the show.

"Coming through!" I yelled, pushing my way through the crowd. "Out of the way, important business."

I tried to get past four women in matching Claire Cleveland fan club T-shirts, but they wouldn't budge.

Their big hair swayed in the wind as the crowd milled around them.

"Excuse me, ma'am," I said, trying to be polite and worm my way past.

"No," said the first woman, an older blonde. "I have been waiting for this night for the last seven months, so don't show up here right before the show opens and expect to be first in line."

"Seven months?" I stopped in my tracks. These people really were crazy.

"We work on the show," Frank tried to reason with her.

"Hmph," said another one of the women. "Nice try."

She turned to one of her friends. "We work on the show," she repeated, in an impression of Frank that was both surprisingly accurate and surprisingly cruel. Then they turned their backs, creating a wall of Claire Cleveland faces staring back at us from their T-shirts. I tried to go around them, but it was no use. The crowd wouldn't let us through. There was something very wrong with these people.

Suddenly the crowd parted, like in one of those nature documentaries, when a shark swims through a school of fish. People were moving out of the way, quickly! The line of women in Claire Cleveland shirts moved apart, and Jason appeared between them, his pink hair shining in the sun.

"Oy!" he shouted. "Come on. Real business going on. Some of us work here, you know. Now move!"

He flashed a smile at us.

"I was out getting lunch, and I saw you two trying to work your way back in," he said. "Figured I'd give you a hand. You have to remember—these aren't people. They're fans. Whole different kettle of fish."

Although he was small—maybe only five feet four inches—there was something about Jason that made people listen. As we followed him, the crowd parted easily before us. It was almost magic. Once we were inside, he told us that Claire and Linden were still rehearsing. He hadn't seen Laurel or Damien all day. Nancy, Bess, and George were "somewhere," but he couldn't get more specific than that.

"We should talk to Claire," I said. "We need to warn her."

"Yeah, but warn her about what?" said Frank. "Until we get some answers from Laurel or Damien, I don't want to go spreading rumors."

"Good point," I agreed. "But maybe she can tell us where they are."

I knocked on the heavy door that led to the rehearsal room. I heard a vague voice respond from inside, and I decided that was my cue to open the door.

"Hi guys!" said Claire, who was brandishing a pistol at a seated Linden. "Come on in!"

She pointed the gun at us.

I threw my hands up in the air.

"Whoa, hey, calm down now," I said, mentally calculating the distance between us. If I tried to tackle her, would she shoot me? I wondered . . .

"Oh, sorry." Claire laughed and dropped the gun on the floor. "Prop gun. My bad."

"That's cool," I said. "Just give me a minute to pry my heart out of my throat."

Claire laughed, but Linden sighed loudly.

"So have you two found anything yet?" he asked. His voice made it clear that he expected the answer to be no.

"We're following some leads," said Frank.

"Sounds like a 'no' to me." Linden laughed and stood up, pacing the room. He seemed on edge, but with his star getting death threats and opening night a few hours away, I could forgive him that.

"We need to talk to a few people. Have you seen Laurel or Damien?"

"Not in hours," said Claire. Linden nodded his agreement. I looked at Frank.

"Claire . . ." I said. "We need you to be careful today, okay?"

Claire nodded, her eyes wide. "Well, I was planning on taking a walk down that abandoned alley next door without telling anyone, but maybe I'll skip that."

She stuck her tongue out at me. It was hard to keep a straight face around her, but I had to impress upon her how serious this was. It was literally life or death.

"Claire, for real," I said, putting my hand on her shoulder. Man, was she warm! "If anything seems suspicious, for any reason, get one of us. Or Nancy."

"Touching," snickered Linden. "But I've got to get ready for tonight. Everyone who's anyone is going to be here. And I've got to go lead a press tour backstage. Unless you need me for anything?"

Frank shook his head. "No, it's okay. But if you see Damien or Laurel, send them our way?"

"Of course," said Linden as he breezed out the door.

"Finally!" said Claire. "He's such a stick-in-the-mud. You get one line wrong, and suddenly you're running lines with him twenty times in a row! He doesn't work any of the other actors this hard."

"Are you ready for tonight?" I asked. I couldn't help thinking that Linden must have decided that Claire needed all the extra rehearsal time. With the whole show basically riding on her, he had to be worried.

"I'm not even going to answer that," she said, taking Linden's chair. "I was *born* ready for this. Tonight is going to be fantastic!"

I have to admit, I was surprised. Claire seemed to be in a great mood, despite the death threats.

"You're not worried?"

"Worried?" Claire laughed. "Ticket sales are through the roof! A scalper is offering tickets on Craigslist for four hundred dollars. And they're in the mezzanine! Earlier today, my agent got a call from some national schools coalition, and they want me to do a public service announcement about standing up to bullies. This is rad!"

Claire clapped her hands with glee, like a kid in a candy store.

"I was asking about the threats, actually," I told her. "Not the show."

"Whatever," she said. "It's just some wacko with too much time on his hands. This stuff happens. Try not to sweat it."

The theme music from her TV show suddenly started playing, and Claire paused to pull her phone from her bag.

"Ugh!" she made a face. "Speak of the devil."

She handed the phone to me. On the screen it said "The opening act will be your final number!"

"It's the same phone number as before," I said. "Quick, Frank, call Vijay."

"Already on it," said Frank. "Hey, Veej, we need you to run a trace on that number we gave you. They just texted Claire."

The room went quiet as Frank waited for Vijay's response. Claire tapped her foot unconsciously, and I wondered if she was more nervous than she let on. The silence stretched out. Finally, Claire couldn't take it any longer.

"Don't bother," she said. "It's probably some sad, Internet crazy in Omaha or something."

"What's that Vijay?" said Frank, putting one hand over his ear. "Okay, got it." He hung up the phone. From his face, I could tell it wasn't good news.

"Whoever texted you shut off their phone pretty quick," he said. "But not before Vijay was able to trace the general location." He paused and looked at Claire. "The text came from Manhattan."

Claire's face froze. A moment later she was laughing and seemed carefree, but I had seen the worry in her eyes. Claire had obviously seen many strange things in her life, but she was smart enough to know that these threats were different.

"Don't worry, Claire," I said. "We're here. You're safe."

Claire opened her mouth, but before she could say anything, a tremendous crash came from outside the door!

BRINGING DOWN THE HOUSE

"I said, what are you doing up here?" Damien growled again, his hand tightening around the saw. He wasn't a big guy, but up in the grid, it didn't matter. One wrong move, and we'd all go plunging off the edge of the walkway. There was no way around him, and he was standing between us and the path back downstairs. We were in trouble.

"We were just exploring!" said George. She took what looked like a nervous step to the side, but I knew she was trying to block Damien from seeing the knot we had just tied. If he knew we'd found his trap, there was no way we could bluff out of this. "I've always been a big techie, and I just wanted to learn more about the backstage stuff."

"I'm fascinated by the light board!" chirped Bess. "Maybe you can show me how it works?"

She smiled one of her big Bess smiles, and I knew she was trying her best to lure him into a false sense of security. She took a step toward him.

"Don't lie to me!" he yelled, brandishing the saw in one hand. "Don't you come any closer."

Damien took a step back, and his heel caught on one of the struts that made up the walkway. He stumbled, and I saw my chance. I lunged forward and yanked the saw from his hand. We wrestled for a second, but I was too strong for him, and in a second, the saw was mine. I tried to pin his arm in a shoulder lock, but he pulled away, just out of reach. As he retreated, his hand caught my sleeve and he pulled, spinning me around. I slammed into the railing, tumbling to my knees.

"Nancy!" someone screamed. I heard the sounds of a struggle above me, but I couldn't make out what was happening. My head was spinning. I put a hand down to steady myself—and nearly plunged off the walkway! I was now balancing on the narrowest section of the path. An inch farther and I'd go right over, down onto the stage below. Far, far below.

I tried to slowly stand, but the saw, which I was still clinging to, was caught on something. I couldn't drop it onto the stage. I pulled, and it came loose with a tearing sound. There was a terrific crash from below. The entire grid shook as though an earthquake had hit. The saw must have been stuck on the rope holding up the plane door. I hoped everyone on the stage survived, but right now, I had to stop Damien. I struggled to my feet.

"Look what you did!" he was yelling. "I knew it was you! You and those guys. Let go of me! It's all your fault! You're the saboteurs."

"Watch out!" Bess yelled, as Damien managed to pull free of her grasp. He turned to run, but I had recovered. I threw myself at him, pinning him against the railing. George grabbed his arms.

"You're going away," I told him as he struggled in our grasp. "For a long time."

"You going to try and kill me, too?" he wailed.

"No," said a voice. I looked up and there were the Hardys. "You're under arrest."

Frank pulled out his ATAC badge.

"Help me!" yelled Damien. "If you're the police, arrest these girls! They're the ones who knocked the plane doors down. They're out to kill Claire!"

His relief was so evident that I had to believe him. He really thought we were the bad guys.

"George, Bess—let him go."

We all backed away, not wanting to be too close if he

made another crazy move. Damien shook his arms out and straightened up. He popped his collar and ran one hand through his hair, which had become a wild poof of curls.

"Please arrest these women," he said, trying to sound calm and professional. "They have been harassing Claire Cleveland."

"Should we arrest this twerp?" Joe asked me.

"No." I shook my head. "I want to hear what he has to say."

"When I came up here, these three . . . ladies . . . perpetrators were clustered around the base of that pole over there," Damien sputtered. It was clear he was trying to talk like the police on television. "That one proceeded to attack me, take my saw, and cut the rope. There is evidence of their misdemeanors all over the place. Look, she's still holding the saw!"

"He makes a good case," Frank winked at me.

"I was holding the saw because I took it from him!" I responded. "George noticed the rope swaying in the wind, and we realized that someone had sawed it nearly in two. I guess he was coming back to finish the job."

"No way!" yelled Damien. "I found that saw at the base of the ladder. It looked like someone dropped it in a hurry, so I was coming to check on things. You don't know how many strange accidents I've had to prevent this last week. This show is cursed!"

"So you weren't coming to look at a certain shrine, were you?"

Damien blushed beet red and looked at his feet.

"Shrine?" said Joe. "Want to fill us in?"

"Someone," I said, nodding in Damien's direction, "has built a little shrine to Claire up here. A picture of her, a lock of her hair, a few stolen things."

"I think his face is enough of a confession," said Frank. "So you were coming up here to finish the job? Kill Claire off during the opening number?"

"No!" screamed Damien. He was suddenly standing up straight again. "I love Claire! Okay, yes, I took some of her stuff. But just little things that she wouldn't miss. I was trying to make a little good luck charm for her. You don't know what it's been like around here these last few weeks. Every day, something goes wrong. Last week I found a razor blade in her dance shoes! Yesterday, someone had stripped the wiring in her dressing room. If I hadn't got an electrician in pronto, it might have burned the whole place down."

Whoa, I thought. If Damien was telling the truth, that meant Claire might be in a lot more danger than we knew!

"And you had nothing to do with any of this?" asked Frank. "You didn't sabotage that plane, or lock me in the basement?"

Damien's face froze with his mouth hanging open.

He looked like he'd just choked on his own tongue.

"I didn't mean to . . . I was just . . . I didn't know you were . . . I was jealous," he finally mumbled. "You show up out of nowhere, and there are all these accidents, and Claire is flirting with you, and I just wanted you to go away. But I never touched that plane! I swear, I would never do anything to hurt Claire."

He jumped forward and grabbed Frank's shirt. I moved to pull Damien off, but Frank held up a hand.

"I love her! I've loved her since the fourth grade, when I saw her in *Melly and Max's Best Day Ever*! You've got to believe me."

Damien had his face pressed close to Frank's, and I was pretty sure he was crying. He was talking fast and a little bit crazy, but what he was saying rang true.

"Working for Claire Cleveland is the only job I ever wanted," he sniffed. "I never thought I would do anything so important in my whole life. I didn't think I'd even get an interview, since I've never worked on Broadway before. And when I spent half the time gushing about Claire, I really thought I'd shot myself in the foot. But Laurel asked me how I felt about her! Arrest me for stealing her stuff if you have to, but just let me be here tonight. I have to protect Claire. Please?"

As I watched, Joe and Frank exchanged a look.

"What exactly did Laurel ask you?" Joe said.

"She wanted to know how all the applicants felt about Claire," said Damien, letting go of Frank. "She said this show was a big deal, and Claire was the star, and we couldn't have anyone on set who didn't really, really love her. I guess that's why she sent the job posting out over the fan club listserv."

"Tell me more about what Laurel said." Frank put his arm around Damien's shoulders. Joe pulled Bess, George, and me aside.

"Madonna was the same way," he whispered. "No experience. Obsessed with Claire."

"That's definitely weird," I responded. "I don't know a lot about showbiz, but I'm pretty sure you have to put in your time before you get to Broadway."

Bess snorted.

"And 'Claire Cleveland Fan Club president' does not count as relevant experience on your resume!" she whispered sharply.

"There's more," Joe whispered. "Frank found a website full of photos and gossip about the show. We're pretty sure Laurel has been the one leaking information! The only thing we don't know is why."

But I knew exactly why she was doing it.

"Money," I said. "That's why."

"But that doesn't make any sense. How does ruining her own show make her money?"

"She's not ruining it," I explained. "Look at it this

way. Say you had a show you weren't all that certain about. Lots of problems you couldn't fix, an expensive and hard-to-please star, people eager to see you fail. So instead of fixing all the problems, you decide to feature them. It's a way of guaranteeing press. And who wouldn't want to see a show where the lead actress might actually be killed onstage? It's morbid and weird, but that's celebrity these days. I bet you every time she blogged about another accident, ticket sales jumped another twenty percent!"

"Hey guys," Frank said, interrupting us. "I think Damien feels pretty bad about what he's done, right?"

Damien nodded his head frantically.

"If he promises to stop stealing Claire's things, I told him we'd let him help us protect Claire tonight. I was going to send him down to tell Linden that everything is okay up here. Then he should go to the rehearsal room and stay with Claire until the moment she goes out onstage. Got it, Damien?"

"Yes, sir!" Damien said.

"That sounds like a good plan to me," I chimed in. "Just don't go picking up any stray saws you see on the way, okay?"

Damien blushed and nodded.

"One thing before you go," said Joe. "Have you seen Laurel?"

"Ms. von Louden said she was going home to change

for the opening," Damien said. "But that was hours ago."

I looked at Frank. "You guys should head to her place. The three—four—of us will look after Claire."

"Better hurry," said Damien. "Curtain goes up in two hours. Well, so long as we can do something about that plane door on the stage. . . ."

CHAPTER **15**

F R A N K

THE THRILL OF THE CHASE!

I was dialing Vijay before we even got out of the theater.

"Hey hey hey," he answered. "How are my favorite sibling detectives? Okay, you're also my only sibling detectives, but that shouldn't—"

"No time, Veej," I cut him off. "I need every scrap of information you have on Laurel von Louden, starting with her home address."

"Thirty-two Beekman Place," he answered instantly. When it came to finding information, Vijay was faster than Google. "It's on the other side of town, between Forty-ninth and Fiftieth Streets, next to the East River."

"Thanks, Vijay. She might be making a run for it."

"I'll alert the authorities as soon as we hang up. And I'll see if I can get you any other useful information on her."

I hung up and turned to Joe. "She's across town. We need a cab, fast!" Quickly I pulled up a map on my phone, just in case we got lost. Beekman Place was a tiny one-way street that only existed for a single block. Very exclusive. Very money.

The crowd was still outside the theater, but we didn't have time to make nice. We pushed through them at high speed.

"I feel like a real New Yorker now!" said Joe, as we battled our way off the sidewalk and on to Forty-Second Street.

"Taxi!" I yelled, jumping off the curb and out into the street, the way everyone else in the city seemed to do it. It always worked in movies. Unfortunately, there wasn't a yellow cab in sight.

"Need a ride?" someone asked beside me.

I turned to find a girl with long dreadlocks standing next to me, leaning against one of those strange pedicabs. It looked like a small horse-drawn carriage, except instead of a horse, the pedicab was powered by a bicycle.

"No," I said. "We've got to get across town fast!"

"Suit yourself," she said. "But the time you'll waste waiting for a taxi at this time of day is way more than the time it'd take me to get you there."

"Fine," said Joe, leaping into her cab. "Thirty-two Beekman Place." He reached down and pulled me in after him. It was like sitting on the smallest, least comfortable couch in the world while someone dragged it down the street attached to their bike—which was pretty much exactly what it was. But we were moving, and that was all that mattered.

"Now, on your right we're going to be coming up on Duffy Square," our dreadlocked driver began to lecture us on New York City sights. "Most people think of all of this as Times Square, however, in truth . . ."

It was amazing to me that someone with such crazy hair could be so . . . boring. Right at that moment, Vijay called me back.

"What are the chances your lady-friend is calling the airport just to check out the weather at JFK?" he said.

"Slim to none," I said.

"It's a bit strange to be headed out of town on opening night, wouldn't you say?" Vijay asked. "But it looks like Ms. von Louden just purchased a first-class, one-way ticket to Buenos Aires. Odd, no?"

"Yup," I agreed. Joe was staring at me with ill-concealed interest. "Veej, hold on, I'm going to put you on speaker. Keep us updated."

I put the phone on the seat between us. "She's headed to the airport."

"Then we need to hurry up," he yelled. "Step on the gas! Or, err . . . pedal to the metal!"

Our driver obediently stopped talking and started

pedaling harder, her back hunching over the bike so she could push with her whole body. The pedicab rushed down the street, flying through Times Square, ducking and dodging between pedestrians. When we hit traffic, she didn't even slow down: She wove in and out of lanes like an Olympic skier in the slalom event.

"Wow," said Joe. "You're definitely getting a big tip!" he yelled to the cabbie. She grinned and pedaled harder.

"You have cash on you, right?" Joe whispered in my ear. "I'm out."

I nodded and put my hand down over my phone, so it didn't hurtle out of the cab.

As we sped across Second Avenue, leaving a long line of honking cars in our wake, Vijay's voice crackled over my phone speaker again.

"Uh, guys, if you don't get there soon, I'm afraid you're going to be performing to any empty house."

"Could we get that in English, Veej?" I asked. We didn't have time for riddles.

"I ran a tap on her house phone, and it looks like Laurel just called her chauffeur."

We were almost there—but even though our pedicab driver was excellent, there was no way she could keep up with a limo. Once Laurel was in that car, we were done for.

"I have an idea!" yelled Joe. "Hey, can you go down Fiftieth Street?" he asked our cabbie, leaning forward.

"Sure thing," she said. "But Beekman Place is one way. In the other direction."

"That's what I'm counting on." Joe smiled.

"What's the plan?" I asked. We were flying up First Avenue now. In a few seconds, we'd be turning onto Beekman Place. I had no idea what Joe had planned.

"Remember that story Nancy told us about her last case?"

"The one with the lieutenant governor?" I vaguely remembered it. Now we were on Fiftieth Street, just half a block from Laurel's place. I hoped we were in time.

"Remember how they stopped his car?"

Beekman Place turned out to be a narrow, tree-lined street. It was beautiful, and if the first thing I saw wasn't Laurel climbing into the backseat of a black town car, I might have really liked it.

"We're too late!" I banged my fist into my leg in frustration.

"No we're not!" Joe shouted. "Stop here!"

The limo pulled slowly away from the curb, but there was nowhere for it to go—the pedicab was in the way, stopped in the middle of the intersection.

"I'm going to have to turn around," our cabbie said. "Sorry about this, guys, but it's hard to make a U-turn in this. This will take a minute."

"Not a problem," said Joe. "I was counting on that."

He hopped out of the pedicab. He looked up at the girl cabbie.

"I'm really, really sorry about this," he said. He pointed at me. "He'll pay you back."

Then Joe took a deep breath, steadied his posture, and kicked the pedicab as hard as he could. The modified bicycle tire collapsed beneath his foot and the whole cab sank onto its side, blocking the street and making it impossible for Laurel's town car to go around. The street was too narrow for the big limo to make a U-turn. Laurel was trapped.

"Hey! What did you do that for? That was not cool man!" Our cabbie started yelling at us. The back door of Laurel's town car flung open, and one stiletto-heeled shoe poked out. We had no time to waste.

"So sorry!" I yelled at the cabbie. I thrust my phone at her. "Here, talk to our manager. He'll pay for all the damages."

I trusted Vijay to think on his feet, and I left him apologizing to our cabbie. He'd probably tell the story he usually used in these situations—that Joe and I were spoiled rich kids out for a joyride in Manhattan. Sometimes I thought Vijay liked that story so much because it made us look bad!

Joe and I ran toward the car. Laurel, in a getaway dress that looked ready to be worn on the red carpet, barely made it two feet before we were on her. I grabbed her arm, ready to tackle her if I had to, but there was no need. She pressed her back against the trunk of the car and slowly sank to the ground, laughing and crying at the same time. She looked more than a little bit crazy. I almost felt sorry for her.

"Laurel?" I said. "Ms. von Louden? Hello?"

Laurel didn't even look up at me, she just pulled a monogrammed handkerchief from her purse and tried to wipe her face. But all she managed to do was smear her makeup like a clown.

"She won't say anything," I told Joe. He picked up her purse and searched inside.

"She won't need to," he said, pulling out a clunky black phone. It was nothing like the slim, sleek smart-phone she'd been tapping away on all week. "I bet I know what we'll find if I check the outgoing messages on this," he said to Laurel. "Now do you want to talk to us?"

"Yes!" she said. "Why not? It'll all come out anyway. Yes! I sent her those messages. Little spoiled brat. She was ruining us, you know?"

"How do you mean?" I asked, squatting on my heels next to her. Her driver had exited the car, but he took one look at Laurel's face and decided to get back inside instead of coming to talk to us. I could only hope he wasn't calling the police.

"Her contract! We were paying her a fortune every

week. We thought with her on the bill, we'd have a guaranteed hit on our hands. So we just put her into the first script we could acquire. But the show was a mess! It took months of work to get it ready, and she refused to renegotiate. She had us over a barrel. Conniving little . . ."

"So you decided to kill her?" I asked.

"No!" screamed Laurel. "I just wanted her to leave. We couldn't fire her, but if she quit, her contract would be null and void. But nothing I did could get her to leave. That girl is made of steel. And then . . ."

"Then what?" Joe prompted. Laurel had broken off and was staring into the distance.

"Somehow, someone learned about the threats. They leaked it to the media. Suddenly, people were interested in the show! We started getting some press. Linden and I . . . we were desperate, you see. If we could make our money back, we figured this might not be a total disaster. So that was the plan. We hired all new crew—people with no experience, crazy fans, anyone we thought might make for good gossip. Any time something went wrong, I tweeted about it, and our press shot through the roof. We actually started selling tickets! But he took it too far. . . ."

Laurel broke off. Her lips quivered and she collapsed into sobs.

"I never meant for this to happen!" she wailed. "I was trying to warn her."

My stomach heaved and my hands broke out in a cold sweat. Whatever Laurel was talking about, I could tell it was bad news.

"Trying to warn who about what? Who went too far? Talk to us, Laurel!"

Laurel broke off crying and grabbed my arm. Her eyes were wide and crazy.

"Tell me it's not too late!"

"Too late for what?" I said. "Tell us!"

She flinched and took a deep breath. She turned her face to the ground as though she were too embarrassed to look at us. Then she started speaking in a fast, quiet whisper.

"It was Linden's idea. I never would have agreed to it but he said I had to. 'We've come so far,' he said. 'The police will never believe you if you turn on me now.'"

"What's he planning, Laurel?" said Joe. "If you tell us, we can still stop him."

"Is she . . . is Claire still alive?" Laurel's voice cracked as she spoke.

"Yes, but she might not be for long. You are the only one who can help us, Laurel."

"You have to stop him!" she yelled, suddenly animated again. "He's paid one of the chorus girls to kill her. Tonight! He said, if she dies during opening night, it will be publicity like no other. We could replace her with some no-name and we'd be raking in the cash. I didn't want to do it! I tried to get her to quit, but she ignored all of my threats. That's why I got this phone, so I could warn her! I didn't know what else to do."

Laurel was crying quietly now, her eyes closed, her head slumped back against the car. All the fight and the crazy had seeped out of her, and she just seemed tired now. Joe pulled a pair of cuffs from his back pocket and slipped one around her wrist. He attached the other to the door handle of the car. She barely seemed to notice.

"Who is it, Laurel?" I grabbed her shoulder and talked to her quietly. "Who did Linden pay off?"

"I don't know," she whispered. "I didn't want to know . . ."

Our former cabbie still had my phone, but luckily, Joe had his in his pocket.

"Nancy!" I heard him yell. "We have a situation."

Quickly, he filled her in on everything we'd learned. Then he was quiet for a minute.

"We'll be there as soon as we can. Be careful!" he said. He listened for a second.

"The curtain's about to go up? There's only one option, then. Nancy, you have to go on in Claire's place! Until we can figure out who the killer is, it's the only way to catch her."

STAGE FRIGHT

As I hung up on Joe, my heart leapt into my throat. I was going to have to go onstage. On opening night. On Broadway! I think I'd had this nightmare before. It was right up there with the one where I showed up at school for final exams and realized I'd missed every day of the semester.

Claire, Damien, Bess, George, and I were all in Claire's dressing room. It wasn't a very large room, and with all of us there, it felt like a sardine can. A very pink sardine can. But at least we were all safe here. Claire was in her costume already, and I could dimly hear the sounds of the audience filling up the theater. It was now or never.

"Claire," I said, putting my hand on her shoulder.

She looked up from the mirror on her vanity, where she'd been checking to make sure her wig was perfect. "You can't go out there."

Behind me, someone gasped. Claire's brow furrowed and her lips pursed. I could tell she was about to argue with me. I cut her off before she could even start.

"Linden's paid someone in the cast to kill you during the first act. We know it's a chorus girl, but not which one. You can't be on that stage with them."

I paused and took a deep breath.

"I'm going to do the opening number."

"No way," said Claire. "This is my opening night!"

"And you'll have it," I said quietly, trying to impress Claire with the seriousness of the situation. "The whole thing—except for the opening number. Would you rather be the famous actress who fooled a would-be assassin and still did the show? Or the famous actress who was murdered while the orchestra was still playing the overture?"

When I put it that way, Claire had to agree. Quickly, she began stripping out of her uniform and getting me into it.

"George, I need you to go up in the grid," I said, as Claire pulled the curly wig down over my head. "I need you to be my eyes and ears. From up there, you should be able to see anyone who might try to make a move on me."

"On it," said George, already rushing toward the door. "But how will I let you know what I see?"

"Leave that to me," said Bess. "Damien, can you get me three of those mics all the techs use?"

"Sure, but why?" I couldn't help but notice that somehow, amid all the chaos of the last few minutes, Damien and Claire had ended up holding hands. *Interesting*, I thought.

"Because we're going to be on a relay. George, you'll keep tabs on the show from above. I'll be backstage. And Nancy—you'll be center stage."

"Don't remind me," I muttered as I quickly began applying makeup. Even as I went over the lines and steps in my head, I was still trying to pretend this wasn't happening.

"What about me?" said Claire. "What can I do?" Damien nodded along with her words.

"Stay right here. Do not open this door for anyone other than us, or Frank and Joe. Do you hear me?"

"I'll stand guard outside!" volunteered Damien.

"No!" said Claire. She pulled Damien closer to her. "I mean, can't you stay inside? With me?"

"Inside, outside—just stay here!" said George. "I can hear the orchestra tuning up. We need to get to our places."

I set my little WWII army cap on my head and looked in the mirror. With the outfit and makeup, even my dad would have had a hard time telling Claire and me apart.

"Let's do this," I said. Damien ran and got us mics, then locked the door behind us when we left. George split off from the group first, heading for the ladder up to the grid. Then Bess found a spot in the backstage left where she could see all of the action onstage (conveniently, I noticed, next to that cute carpenter, Tim). Then I was standing alone above the tiny tape *X* that marked Claire's starting position for the show.

All around me, actors in uniforms and period costumes were filing in. From the grid, a model of a French country home slowly descended onto center stage. The opening number was a large group dance sequence that was supposed to portray the fall of France to the Nazis. I was thankful that it wasn't a song in which Claire—I mean, I—had to sing. But there were a lot of steps to remember. *Ball, kick, change, jump* . . . I repeated in my head.

The curtain was still down, but I could hear the audience growing quiet. I looked at the faces around me. Perfectly made-up, in crisp Nazi uniforms, any one of them could have been the killer.

Suddenly, a pair of violins began to play the opening notes of the score. The audience burst into applause.

From the sound of it, there were a lot of people out there.

"Break a leg, Nancy," George said over my mic.

"Preferably, someone else's," Bess added.

Then the curtain was rising and the lights were shining down. All around me, dancers burst into action. The uniformed Nazis grabbed the Parisians and danced them menacingly off the stage. Some dancers dodged and wove around the Nazis, portraying the men and women of the French Resistance, who had plagued the Nazis long after the French government had surrendered. Despite the danger, the rousing music and the elaborate dancing filled me with emotion. I let the character of Nancy Wake fill me as I took my opening steps, ducking past two Nazis who pretended to grab me. One artful slow-motion spin kick later, and they were both down on the ground. The spotlight followed me as I dove across the stage.

And the people applauded! The audience seemed to be into every move I made. I could see why Claire loved her job so much. But I couldn't let myself get carried away. I had steps to remember, and a killer to foil.

"Looking good from up here," came George's voice in a burst of static. Taken by surprise, I stumbled, crashing into one of the Resistance fighters, a handsome older man. He grabbed me gracefully and spun me to the side so effortlessly it looked as though we had planned it all along.

"All clear from my angle," Bess chimed in. But I shook my head, trying to ignore them. Something about my misstep had triggered my memory.

What was it Madonna had told Joe? Something about the backup dancers being less in sync than she was. It was one of the Nazis, she'd said! The blond one! A blond Nazi had nearly knocked Madonna down during rehearsal. It wasn't much to go on, and there were a lot of blond dancers dressed as Nazis. I was grasping for straws, hoping to find the killer before it was too late.

I tried to watch the dancers as they dipped and whirled, but it was hard to keep track of them, they moved so gracefully. All except for one. There was a tall blonde in the back row who seemed to be out of step. In fact, she seemed to be trying to fight her way across the crowded stage toward me!

"George, backstage left—no, right—no, left! That girl, the tall blonde in the Nazi uniform. Do you see her?"

"Which one? Wait, I think I got her. Seems a little lost?"

"Is she trying to make her way toward me, or am I crazy?" I pirouetted around a "dead" girl, pulling off my jacket as I went. This part of the dance was meant to symbolize how I went underground and became a spy.

I was supposed to change out of my uniform and into civilian clothing, piece by piece. But I had bigger issues on my mind.

"Roger that, Nancy," came Bess's voice. "She's definitely tracking you. Do you want us to—Nancy! She's making a run for you."

I turned and there she was, all six-feet of her blond, muscular, uniformed dancer's body running flat-out at me. Her hand was reaching for her holster. Somehow, I doubted she had a prop gun like the rest of us.

Without thinking about it, I yanked the fake gun from my hip and threw it at her, end over end.

Smack!

I lucked out, and the handle of the pistol slammed directly into her nose. The audience gasped with surprise as blood spurted out. Though the actress stopped in her tracks, she was still trying to get her gun out. I ran at her, full speed, trusting the real dancers to get out of my way.

I slammed into the girl, my shoulder hitting her in the chest, just below her arm. She'd finally succeeded in freeing her gun, and it was pointing right at me when I struck.

We slammed to the ground in a heap. I heard a tremendous roar as the gun went off, and something kicked hard against my stomach. There was the sound of shattering glass, and then a rain of shards fell down around us. The blast had nearly deafened me. I looked out at the audience. I could tell they were screaming because their mouths were open, but I couldn't hear a thing.

That's when the rest of the lights went out.

CHAPTER 17

JOE

THE FINAL CURTAIN

"You don't understand. You have to let us inside!" I
yelled. Frank and I had run all the way from Laurel's
apartment to the theater, and we weren't about to let
some stupid security guys stop us now. We'd made it
through the first double doors and into the lobby, but
there we'd run out of luck.

The stupid security guys had their own thoughts
about the matter.

"No," said the shorter of the two guards, who was
approximately seven feet four million inches tall. I felt
like I had to look up just to see his belt. And he was the
smaller of the two.

"No one is allowed through these doors until intermission," rumbled the other guard, who sounded like a truck engine when he spoke.

"Please," said Frank. "This is a matter of life and—"

But before he could finish, a shot rang out from inside the theater. Everyone in the lobby froze for a second. Then the door burst open and the black-tie crowd inside came rushing out. Ties flashing, gowns flapping, they were a raging river of riches that the security guards could not hope to stop. In fact, all the guards could do was huddle against the wall and hope not to get crushed—which left an opening for us!

"Come on," Frank yelled, grabbing my arm and pulling me into the theater. It was hard going, fighting against the terrified ticket holders. Luckily (or perhaps not), this wasn't our first time in a rioting crowd. It felt a little bit like one of those video games where you have to jump at just the right moment to make it through a moving opening.

Of course, it was made more difficult by the fact that I was on my cell phone, frantically dialing Bess, George, and Nancy. On the third try, Bess picked up.

"What's going on?" I yelled. "Where are you?"

"I'm backstage! Claire is fine. Nancy found the killer and tackled her onstage, but she managed to get off a shot. It must have shorted the lighting system, because it's pitch black in here! I can't find Nancy."

"We're on our way. Keep an eye out for Linden!"

We finally pushed our way out of the lobby and into the theater. Sure enough, it was lit only by the dim red glow of the emergency exit signs, and a few smart phones being used as flashlights.

"Nancy might be injured. She's somewhere onstage, but Bess can't find her," I told Frank. I dodged past an older woman in a sequined black dress and leapt over a row of seats. Slowly, we made our way up the central aisle toward the stage. I looked back to check on Frank, and as I did, I slammed into someone running out of the theater.

"Linden!" I yelled. He froze. I tried to pretend I didn't know he was the guilty one, but the shock must have been clear on my face, because he turned the other way, pushed a young girl down on the ground in front of me, and took off.

"Stop him!" I yelled, but no one paid any attention.

"You stop him," said Frank, who was a row behind me. "I'll find Nancy. Go!"

That was all I needed to hear. If Frank said he would take care of Nancy, he would. And that left me to do what I do best: Stop the bad guy.

The girl was already stumbling to her feet, and I saw she wasn't injured. I pushed past her with a quick apology and followed Linden. Even in the dim light, he was easy to spot because no one else was running *toward* the stage.

I tracked him to within twenty feet of the stage. There was no audience left here, and he had nowhere to run.

"Stop!" I yelled. "Turn yourself in and this will go a whole lot better on you."

But Linden didn't even slow down. He ran full speed at the stage, then vaulted up onto it.

"Dang!" I huffed to myself as I hustled to keep up with him. "Why are these preppy killers *always* former athletes? I bet he was on some sort of brainiac team like debate or chess."

Not that I couldn't keep up with him. As I bounced onto the stage, I watched him slip out into the wings. I hesitated for a second—should I stay and look for Nancy? But if we didn't catch Linden now, chances were he'd be long gone by the time the police came. I had to trust George, Bess, and Frank. I raced after Linden.

It was even darker backstage than in the theater itself. I saw a few people half-hidden in the shadows, but none looked like Linden. I stopped and stood still, waiting for my eyes to adjust. Eventually, he would have to make a move.

A groaning noise came from my left, then the crash of a metal door being flung closed. Linden was headed into the subbasement! I raced across the darkened area and yanked the fire door open. I jumped down the steps two at a time. Somewhere ahead of me I could hear Linden crashing through the prop storage rooms. Either he had all the grace of a steamroller, or he was actively trying to knock everything down around him.

The subbasement was eerie at any time—all those odd pieces of giant scenery and weird props jumbled together in the dark. But when chasing a would-be murderer, it was downright scary. It didn't help that the narrow aisle that once ran the length of the room was now filled with fallen props. I was Joe Hardy though—I wasn't about to let fear slow me down! My bet was that he was hiding somewhere among all this stuff, waiting to ambush me. If he thought he could trick a member of ATAC, he had another think coming.

I jumped over a broken column that must have been left over from a Greek tragedy, when a face appeared in the darkness.

"Hi-yah!" I said, punching Linden right in the head.

"Oww!" I howled, as my hand hit the plaster mask square in its really hard, not-at-all-fleshlike face. That was definitely going to swell up. The mask, at least, had the good grace to collapse into a million pieces, which made me feel a little better.

"Linden!" I yelled into the darkness. "I'm going to find you. We know everything. You might as well give up now!"

I was answered by silence, followed by a loud series of crashes deeper in the subbasement.

"Why do I even bother?" I mumbled to myself as I climbed over a giant pumpkin made out of foam. "They never do it the easy way."

It took a long while to make my way over, under, and around all of the trash that Linden had thrown in my path, but I relentlessly tracked him farther into the storage rooms. Finally, the hallway ended in an open door. Judging from the broken statue of a bear lying in front of the room, Linden was in there. Cautiously, I stepped inside.

The subbasement must have extended beyond the walls of the theater, because this room was so tall it would have hit the orchestra pit if we were still below it. It was here that the biggest props were stored: towering marionettes that looked like they belonged to the children of giants, a black obelisk with creepy red runes carved into it, and an entire wall of shelves that ran up to the ceiling, holding every conceivable kind of light and prop you could imagine. Aside from my panting breath, the room was still and silent.

"Linden?" I said, stepping gingerly deeper into the

room. It was darker here than in the rest of the sub-basement. I wished I'd paused to find the light switches back at the entrance, but it was too late now.

I walked into the center of the room, far away from any of the giant props Linden might be hiding behind. There was an energy, a presence in the room—I could tell he was here, but for the life of me, I couldn't figure out where. Over by the wall of shelves, I heard something skitter.

"Come on, man," I said, turning to face the sound. "Let's just stop this. We have Laurel in custody, there's nothing you can do."

The noise came again, louder this time. It was like metal pushing against metal, and it sent a painful shiver down my spine. Whatever Linden was up to, it couldn't be good. Was it possible there was another exit down here? Was that the sound of a rusted door being pushed open?

I crept closer to the props, trying to stay alert for any sudden movements. There was no way Linden was getting out of here, not on my watch. High up on the shelves, something shifted. I looked up, and there he was!

"Linden!" I yelled. "Come down here!"

But Linden ignored me. He was sitting on one of the tall shelves, fiddling with something against the wall.

"Sorry, kid," Linden called down. "But I'm afraid this show is about to become a tragedy."

Linden kicked out as hard as he could, pounding the wall with both of his feet at the same time. The shelves tipped and pulled away from the walls. That's what he was doing, I realized: He was removing the screws that held the shelves in place. A ton of lights and props was about to come crashing down on my head!

I raced back the way I had come, hurtling toward the bright door and my only chance of survival. The shelves were so big that they moved slowly, but they were quickly picking up speed. From high above, large pieces of metal began to rain down as the heaviest objects rolled off the now tilting shelves. I sprinted through the deadly hail. Glancing up I saw the shelves rushing toward me from above. I was just a few feet from the door! I threw myself forward with all my might, just barely clearing the door frame before a humongous prop smashed into the ground where I had been standing.

I hit the ground head first and rolled. My hands were skinned and my shoulder felt like I might have dislocated it, but I'd made it out alive.

There was a roar as the shelves hit the other wall in the room and an avalanche of stuff smashed to the ground. Great clouds of dust flew up and the echoes of the crash reverberated through the subbasement. But when the echoes stopped and the dust settled, the room was as quiet as a grave.

I poked my head in. The room was unrecognizable. It looked like a junkyard. I pitied whomever's job it would be to clean this all up—Damien, I bet.

One of the giant puppets had collapsed into a heap right by the door. As I watched, it began to move and groan.

"Mr. von Louden, how good of you to join me!" I said, as I pushed aside one giant arm to reveal a stunned, but basically unhurt, Linden.

He shook his head, clearly still confused from the fall. I patted him down, checking for injuries and weapons. Amazingly, he didn't seem to have either. I slipped a handcuff around his wrist and helped him to his feet.

"I want you to know, there is a very special seat reserved for you tonight," I told Linden as I led him out through the basement. "It's in the back of a police car! I really hope you like it."

"Look," said Linden, his voice sounding desperate and dry. "If this is about money, I can get you money. I have a lot of it. You don't even know, kid!"

"This isn't about money," I said, as I kicked open the door to the backstage. "It's about justice."

To my relief, the first people I saw backstage were Nancy and Frank, handcuffing a crazy-looking woman in a Nazi uniform.

"Look!" said Frank. "Between us we have a matched set."

"Nancy!" I couldn't help but shout with joy. "You're okay!"

"Barely," she responded, holding up her wig to show me where the bullet had torn the hair off one side of it. "Should we bring these two out onto the red carpet?"

"Let's!" I said, taking her arm gallantly.

18

OPENING NIGHT, TAKE TWO

"Claire! Look over here!" the paparazzi yelled, as Claire walked by in a fantastic green gown. She waved, then caught sight of Nancy, Joe, Bess, George, and I, and added a wink. Then she was gone, back into the theater for opening night, take two. She'd invited us to walk the red carpet with her, but we had decided it was best for everyone if we kept a low profile.

"So she's taking over the entire show?" Bess asked, sounding impressed.

"She bought out Linden and Laurel," I answered. "Apparently there was a clause in her contract that gave her first option on buying the show, should they fold. And boy, did they ever fold!"

"By noon on the day after we captured Linden,

she'd replaced half the cast and two-thirds of the crew!" added Joe. "Turns out she's a smart business woman, too."

Only a week had passed since we'd captured Linden and Laurel, but it had been a century in the lifetime of *Wake*. The press attention had been incredible—Claire had been on the cover of every paper around the world. Ticket sales went through the roof—and then continued going! Rumor had it the show was sold out for the next year. It was the hottest ticket on Broadway, and Claire was the hottest star . . . and producer . . . and director!

"We should get inside," said Nancy. "I'm excited to see the show from the other side of the stage this time!"

"So your fifteen minutes of fame haven't changed you?" teased George. "You're not leaving River Heights for the bright lights of the big city?"

"Hardly!" laughed Nancy. "If I never have to go onstage again, it'll be too soon."

"Hey! Hey guys! Hey!"

Someone was pushing their way through the crowd to us. Whoever it was wormed their way through hordes of cameramen and adoring fans, and we could track their progress by the sound of apologies. Finally, Damien burst out in front of us, his billowing curls atop a full tuxedo.

"Hey man, looking good!" Joe said, slapping him five. "Got the night off from the show?"

"Yeah," he said. "Actually, Claire asked me to accompany her."

He blushed beet red and stared at his feet.

"Like, on a date?" Bess asked.

"I guess so," Damien mumbled, but the giant smile on his face told the whole story.

"That's great. For both of you!" I clapped him on the shoulder. He was a little strange, but he was a good guy in the end. And maybe a celebrity like Claire needed someone like Damien—having him in the background let her shine all the more, and he seemed more than happy with that role.

As we took our seats in the theater, I looked around with a sense of satisfaction. Another case solved!

And as an added bonus: With the new cast, the show wasn't half bad!

CAROLYN KEENE
NANCY DREW

Secret Sabotage

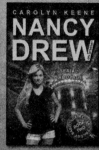
Serial Sabotage

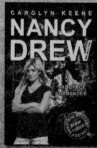
Sabotage Surrender

Secret Identity

Identity Theft

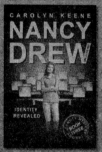
Identity Revealed

Model Crime

Model Menace

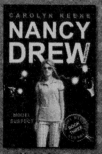
Model Suspect

INVESTIGATE THESE THREE THRILLING MYSTERY TRILOGIES!

FRANKLIN W. DIXON

THE HARDY BOYS

Undercover Brothers®

**INVESTIGATE THESE TWO ADVENTUROUS MYSTERY TRILOGIES
WITH AGENTS FRANK AND JOE HARDY!**

#28 Galaxy X

#29 X-plosion!

#31 Killer Mission

#32 Private Killer

#30 The X-Factor

#33 Killer Connections

**From Aladdin
Published by Simon & Schuster**

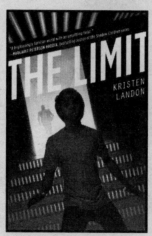
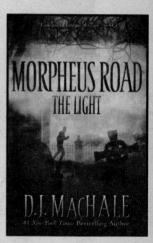

The truth is always closer than you think. . . .